SUMMER OF SALT

SUMMER OF SALT

KATRINA LENO

HARPER TEEN
An Imprint of HarperCollinsPublishers

HarperTeen is an imprint of HarperCollins Publishers.

Summer of Salt
Copyright © 2018 by Katrina Leno
www.epicreads.com

Library of Congress Control Number: 2018933351
ISBN 978-0-06-249362-0

Typography by Alison Klapthor
18 19 20 21 22 PC/LSCH   10 9 8 7 6 5 4 3 2
❖
First Edition

to Shane
who has his own magic

SUMMER OF SALT

I.

It was many and many a year ago,
In a kingdom by the sea.

from "Annabel Lee"
by Edgar Allan Poe

SUMMER SOLSTICE

On the island of By-the-Sea you could always smell two
things: salt and magic.

The first was obvious. It came crashing ashore in the blue
waves; it sat heavy and thick in our hair and our clothes; it
stained our bedsheets and made our pillows damp.

The second—the scent of magic—was harder to pin
down.

It floated behind my mother as she carried a woven basket out to the herb garden in the middle of the night (when
picked under moonlight, rosemary became so much more
than just something that goes well with eggs).

It gathered up in the corners of the Fernweh Inn, mixed
with the dust and the cobwebs that collected in the guest
rooms during the nine months the inn sat (mostly) empty.

And it poured off my sister on the night of the summer solstice, when she stepped up onto the ledge of my

attic bedroom window and unceremoniously pushed herself away, jumping into the night air with all the grace of a poorly trained ballerina.

Oh—don't worry.

She'll be fine.

Of all the stories about my family, the Fernweh women on the island of By-the-Sea, there are two that no one will ever forget. One is the story of how my sister, Mary, and I were born. And the other is the story of the summer we turned eighteen. This summer.

You would never know by looking at my sister that she was the type of girl who could jump from a fourth-story window and float gently to the ground on a warm and windless summer night, landing perfectly between two of my mother's enormous, prized-possession bleeding hearts, trampling not a single blade of grass beneath her bare feet. And yet here we were: A warm and windless summer night. My sister's dress floating around her like a ghost made out of cotton and lace. A fall that should have killed her. A fall that *would* have, if she weren't a Fernweh. My mother's bleeding hearts, untouched, and my sister dropping her sandals on the grass and sliding into them while looking back up at me, an obnoxiously pleased expression on her face, the scent of magic so strong and sharp (like ashes, like shadows, like dirt) that I actually sneezed.

"Bless you!" she called up merrily.

From above, leaning out of the window, I rolled my eyes.

"You're so fucking dramatic," I said.

Mary kissed the air in my general direction.

It took me a few minutes longer to make it down to the grass; we couldn't all float through the summer air. I had to crawl down the lattice that ran up the side of the house, avoiding the thorns of the roses that vined skyward and always made my bedroom smell so sickly sweet. When I finally jumped the last few feet and landed beside her, she had lain down in the grass. She was pretending to be asleep.

"Asshole," I said, and kicked her with the toe of my sandaled foot.

"Jealous," she replied.

"Joke's on you when you get a grass stain on your ass."

"Mom has grass-stain potion," Mary said, and held her hand out to me. I grabbed it hard and pulled her up. She smelled like cinnamon as she smiled at me. "Doesn't this just feel like a night of limitless possibility?" she said, suddenly serious, holding her arms open to the night like she could embrace it.

"Sure, Mary. Whatever you say."

She laughed and pushed me away, and I followed her as she turned and darted across the lawn. I paused at the edge of our property, turning only once to see how creepy the Fernweh Inn looked at night. It was all shadows and things that caught the corner of your eye. Real stuff of ghost stories. I'd always loved it.

"Keep up, Georgina," Mary called as we made our way down Bottle Hill and away from the ocean, toward the center of our island.

Oh, By-the-Sea, our home: just a handful of people with their own presumably good reasons for wanting to live on the grayest and rainiest and arguably most depressing island this side of our great mainland. (This side was east. I imagine if this side were west it would be all sunshine and palm trees and tan, muscular boys with wet suits rolled down to their waists, carrying surfboards on their shoulders as they walked barefoot down the sides of small coastal highways.)

"This is pointless. Everything is pointless," I said. I wore shorts, and my legs were already being eaten alive by mosquitoes. "Did you bring a citronella candle?"

"Oh yes, I'm keeping it in my bra," Mary said. She stopped and waited for me. "Why are you being such a grump?"

"Bonfires are pointless."

"You've already established that *everything* is pointless. I assumed bonfires fell under that umbrella."

"They do."

"What's really bothering you, my poor little grumpy sister?"

We'd reached Main Street, the longest street in

By-the-Sea. It ran north to south and cut the island in half down the middle. You could get all the way from Bottle Hill to the ferry dock on this road. I stood in the middle of it, staring down into the darkness that was punctuated every hundred feet or so by a streetlamp.

In a little over two months, Mary and I would take this road all the way to the docks. We'd board the ferry for the first time in our lives and take it to the mainland. I was going to a small college just far enough from the ocean that for the first time in my life I wouldn't be able to smell salt. Mary would get on a plane and fly south. Her school was on the very tip of the mainland, right on the water. She was tied to the water, my sister. Moods like tides, temper like a hungry shark.

"Georgie?" Mary asked, when a few moments had passed and I still hadn't moved from the middle of the road. Not like there was any *reason* to. We'd counted once; there were fewer than forty cars on By-the-Sea, and we were almost guaranteed to run into none of them at this time of night.

"Just thinking," I said.

"About . . . ?"

"College, I guess."

Mary made a noise in the back of her throat that meant something like "Really? This again?" and at the same time conveyed how unlikely it was that we had come from the same place, the same womb. At the same time, even.

Sometimes I wondered about that myself. I mean, we looked nothing alike. Mary was a blond, and I was a brunette. Mary had brown eyes, and I had green. Mary liked bonfires, and I thought they were pointless. Mary was going far away to a college on the water, and I was having heart palpitations in the middle of the road thinking about a simple little ferry ride.

"Are you still worried about that?" Mary asked. "Georgina, you're going to be fine. You're the smartest person in our class, everyone loves you, and there are bound to be more girls who like girls over there than there are here. It's a simple numbers game."

"Well, at least you have your priorities straight," I said.

"Kissing is important. You've only kissed one person in your entire life. That's weird."

"I think it's weirder that you're methodically making your way through every boy on this very small island."

"God, you *are* a grump," Mary said.

As we spoke, Mary had gradually floated higher and higher into the air. She was a solid five inches off the ground now, and I didn't think she even realized it. My sister had always been lazy about her powers—she went through week-long periods where she practiced diligently, trying to figure out how to control them, learning how to direct her body through the air, but more often than not, she couldn't be bothered.

It worried me. It was one thing trying to keep my sister's

powers a secret from a tiny island, but what would it be like for her to try and hide them from the entire mainland? From her university? From her new roommate?

"Mary," I said sternly, pointing at her feet.

She rolled her eyes and gradually sank back to earth. "There's no one around."

"That's not the point. You know you're supposed to be trying to control it."

"I can't think about it every second of every day," she said, crossing her arms over her chest.

"Let's just get this over with," I said.

I pushed past her, sure of my footing even in the darkness, because I knew the way by heart, because I knew every single way on this island, every single rock or fallen branch that might trip me up. You could walk from one end to the other in two hours, and that's if you were really taking your time.

We weren't going far. The Beach was a fifteen-minute walk from our house. That was the official, in-the-touristbook name for where we were going, one of six beaches on By-the-Sea. (Yes, there was a tourist book for our tiny island. It was made and printed by Willard Jacoby, and I don't think he'd ever sold a single copy.) The Beach was the smallest of the six, a little cove popular with the locals and unpopular with the tourists because of a series of signs warning of frequent shark attacks. The signs, while a blatant lie designed to keep the Beach tourist-free, were incredibly effective; they featured sunblock-nosed stick figures in bathing suits missing arms or legs or huge chunks of their torsos.

The bonfire was held on the Beach every year on the summer solstice. School had been out for a month already, but this was the official start of summer and By-the-Sea's singularly minded two-month tourist season.

The island's population of young people, including the thirty-six of us who made up that year's graduating class, collected on the Beach, drank summer punch, vomited into the waves, and skinny-dipped. I had gone every year since I was thirteen, and this would be my last one. We were done now, Mary and I. Graduated. Elevated. Voilà.

I was only here because of her. She loved this sort of thing. She was born for oceanside bonfires, long gauzy dresses and uncombed hair, the scent of salt like a blanket you can't peel off your skin. She was born for the smell of water, for the way it sank into your bones, stained your skin, dyed your blood a deep, salty blue.

Me, I could never see waves again and be perfectly fine with that.

Mary linked her arm through mine and pulled me against her side, trapping me. "Just so I can adequately prepare myself, how long is your little mood going to last?"

"We've just been to so many of these. I don't really see the point in one more. Especially when we have to be up at the crack of dawn tomorrow."

"Georgie, can't you just live a little? I mean—this is the first night of the rest of your life!"

"But . . . you could say that about every night. Like, every night is the first night of the rest of your life. Because the present is always the present and the only thing in front of us is the rest of our lives."

"Here, I brought this for you because I knew you'd be like this," she said, pulling a small silver flask from her bra.

"Wait, so do you actually have a citronella candle in there?"

"It's the cinnamon stuff you like. *You're welcome.*"

She took a big swig and then handed it to me, shaking her head from side to side like a dog, with her tongue hanging out and everything.

"Georgie, just think about it," she continued. One sip of cinnamon whiskey and her eyes had already gotten all glossy. "In a couple months we'll just be *gone,* you know? This is really it. One last summer on By-the-Sea. One last summer together."

I sipped from the flask. Mary unhooked her vise grip on my arm and took my hand instead. She was swaying a little, which made me think she'd already had her fair share of cinnamon whiskey before she'd knocked on my bedroom door.

"Are you happy at all?" she asked tentatively.

"Of course I'm happy. Why wouldn't I be happy?"

"Oh, I don't know. Sometimes you just find reasons not

to be." She kissed the back of my hand. We'd reached the edge of the Beach. My sister slipped out of her sandals and held them with one finger over her shoulder.

The bonfire's flames were already dangerously high. The people around it were like little human-shaped spots of darkness against the fire. I tried not to let Mary's words into my heart: *sometimes you just find reasons not to be.* If that were true, then Mary's own vice was that she sometimes found the meanest observations and let them fall off her tongue like they were nothing.

"I *am* happy," I said, but I didn't think she heard me. She was preening: running her hands through her hair and adjusting her dress.

"Gimme," she said, holding out her hand. I gave her the flask, and she took another massive sip. "Okay. Don't go far." And she handed the flask back to me and took off running.

I was expecting that. I watched her go until I could no longer distinguish her from the other dark blobs of people.

It occurred to me that I could leave, that I could go back home and sleep for a few hours and then come out again and find her as the sun was rising, lead her home while she floated like a balloon above my head, my hand wrapped tightly around her ankle so I wouldn't lose her to the last few fading stars.

That was the extent of her powers: my sister could float.

She was, of course, hoping they evolved eventually, that

one day she'd be able to get more than a few feet off the ground, but so far, no flying, just floating.

It was a rare gift, but not unheard of among Fernweh women. We had a great-great-aunt who could fly on a God's-honest broom. We had another aunt, farther back, who never actually touched the ground; her feet were always about an inch from the soil she glided on.

And then there was Annabella.

Every year, from late June to late August, By-the-Sea played host to the rarest bird in the entire world: the Eastern Seaborn Flicker.

Although nobody actually called her that. They called her what my great-great-great-maybe-another-great-grandmother, Georgina Fernweh (my namesake, yes), the woman who'd discovered the new species, had called her: Annabella's Woodpecker.

Named after her twin sister, Annabella, who had gone missing around the same time the bird had shown up.

Her twin sister, who had started out being able to float and had, after years of practice, perfected the art of flying.

I'm sure stranger things have happened in my family than a woman possibly-maybe-probably turning into a bird.

But how else could you explain it? The same bird showing up every year, for three hundred years or so, with the same markings and the same coloring and the same mannerisms. Coming back to visit its home. Coming back, perhaps, to say hi to its living relatives (and even the dead ones, buried in the Fernweh tomb on the island's only cemetery).

Of course, the ornithologists and enthusiasts that studied her insisted that a bird with a three-hundred-year lifespan was impossible, and that the more likely explanation was that there just wasn't that much variation between individual units of the species.

They said things like that, *individual units of the species.*

They also said things like, *You should probably at least call it Annabella's Flicker,* to which my great-great-whatever-grandmother was like, *You should probably let me name this rare bird anything I damn well want because she's on my property and, if you piss me off, I'll build a very tall fence.*

And just like every summer, the Fernweh Inn would open tomorrow, and the birdheads would flock to the island in droves. Oh, By-the-Sea, island of salt and sand and rain and magic and one single solitary bird that made our tiny little chunk of rock—which would have been otherwise entirely overlooked by the rest of the world—absolutely famous (at least in certain ornithological circles).

I was rather fond of Annabella.

Not everybody had their own personal island mascot, and she was ours.

And she was a Fernweh, to boot. We Fernwehs had to stick together.

Even those of us without any powers.

Like me.

It was a well-established thing in Fernweh history: that all Fernweh women found their particular gifts by their eighteenth birthday. I had a great-great-aunt who had discovered her powers of teleportation (she could zap herself to anywhere on the island, but she couldn't zap her clothes, so it ended up being a very risqué gift) at the age of four, and she proceeded to use them gleefully, scaring her siblings and parents half to death by popping up in the strangest places. I had yet another great-great-aunt who hadn't discovered her powers of telepathy until she was seventeen and a half.

There seemed to be no rhyme or reason.

Mary and I would be turning eighteen at the end of the summer, and here I was: still resolutely unmagical while Mary had been floating since birth.

I slid my sandals off and walked down toward the water.

I found Vira ankle-deep in ocean, holding her long skirt up around her knees.

"Hi," I said, joining her.

"You smell like cinnamon."

I handed her the flask. At this rate, it would be gone before the midnight rush. (The midnight rush was all who had a mind to take off their clothes and run screaming into the water. I did not have a mind to. Mary was unpredictable; she could go either way.)

Vira took a sip of the flask and smacked her lips

exaggeratedly. She handed the flask back to me and I took the long, last sip.

Vira like Elvira. My best friend, of the non-twin variety. Shoulder-length hair the color of coal and slate-gray eyes. If you actually called her Elvira, she was known to mix crushed-up sleeping pills into your milkshake at Ice Cream Parlor, where she worked. When you woke up, you had Sharpied penises on your cheeks.

"We missed you today," Vira said.

Book club. Consisting of me, Vira, Eloise, Shelby, and Abigail. We met in the back corner of Used Books, which was owned by Eloise's mother.

"*Wuthering Heights* is a terrible book," I said.

"You got to pick the last one."

"Right, and who doesn't love a good *Bell Jar*?"

"You have to stop picking Sylvia Plath. It's making everyone cry."

"It wasn't all *Wuthering Heights*, anyway. I had to help my mom get the inn ready," I explained.

"Ah, the massive influx. All booked?"

"All booked. Check-in's at twelve tomorrow. You're welcome to come and help, Mom said the more the merrier."

"I have to be at the parlor," Vira said. "You know how those birdheads like their ice cream."

Ah, did I know a thing or two about those birdheads.

Behind us a bunch of our drunken peers fell gently into song. It was a sort of island staple, a dark and moody tune that had been around forever. Nobody knew its origins, but everybody knew it. It was what you hummed to yourself on the walk home from school, in the shower, right before you fell asleep. It was one of those songs that entered your brain and never let you forget it.

On By-the-Sea, you and me will go sailing by
On waves of green, softly singing too.
On By-the-Sea, you and me will be forever young
And live together on waves of blue.

It went on like that for many verses, dozens of voices all singing low and slow. The effect, I had to admit, was rather somber. I got goose bumps down my arms that I tried to hide from Vira. Neither of us was singing, but both of us were listening intently. The bonfire warmed the already warm night, and we took a step deeper into the freezing water to even out our body temperature.

We were joined after a minute by Eloise and Shelby, drunk and giggly, and then by Abigail, stoned and serious. The cinnamon whiskey was gone, and we all looked out at the sky, where the clouds were parting to reveal a big, heavy moon.

Abigail took a step deeper into the water, held her hands

up to the sky, and said, "I can't feel my skin anymore."

Shelby laughed and said, "Jesus, Abs, how much did you smoke?"

This side of the island faced west, and I looked out as far as I could, straining my eyes against the inky darkness, trying to see the mainland.

It was no use, of course. Even on the clearest of days, the sunniest of mornings, you could only just make out the shore. In this darkness, I could see only the dots of stars, the shadowy outline of bodies. The bonfire was bright, yes, but it also made the rest of the night somehow darker.

I felt hands around my waist and knew it was my sister by the dark smell of impossibility.

"Are you having fun?" she asked.

Nobody was paying attention; everyone was in their own little world, and that's why I didn't worry much when I felt her arms start to tug upward, sensed her feet leaving the sand behind me. I turned around to face her and placed my hands heavily on her shoulders.

"Get a grip," I whispered.

"Oh, shoot," she said, and splashed back into the water. "I didn't mean to."

"Are you ready to go home?"

"Are you kidding me? Nobody's even gotten naked yet. We have to dance naked under the solstice moon, Georgina, it's tradition."

"Well, you can get naked without me," I said.

"Just give it another half hour or so and I'll go with you. Please? Don't make me walk home by myself."

"Ugh, fine."

Vira turned around. "Hi, Mary."

"Hi, Vira."

"Are you getting naked?"

"Yeah. You?"

"I guess so. I wore my good underwear."

"I wore a bathing suit," Eloise chimed in, lifting her dress to reveal a dark-green one-piece with a skirt.

Abigail took a blanket out of an enormous straw bag she'd brought with her and spread it out. Squeezing, all six of us managed to fit.

My sister indeed got naked not long after that, and together with Vira (in her underwear), Eloise (in her bathing suit), and Shelby and Abigail (both also naked), she went charging into the great blue sea. Most of the Beach had, actually, except for me and a few other people too far away to identify.

It wasn't that I didn't *like* swimming. I just preferred the warm blanket, the bonfire blazing nearby, the inky darkness of the sky.

I guarded our blanket, my sister's clothes, and Abigail's glass pipe. ("This belonged to my great-aunt Dee, okay, so be careful with it and help yourself.")

I watched the teenagers of By-the-Sea run and jump into the freezing-cold water and thought about how many of them would be leaving for the very first time in September. After a few minutes, Colin Osmond folded his exceptionally long legs into pretzels and sat down next to me, deftly maneuvering his way around the many bras and undies and shoes that littered the blanket. We'd gotten to know each other when I'd dated his sister, Verity, last year, and we'd remained friendly after we'd broken up.

"Never understood this," Colin said. "That water is *cold*."

"Freezing," I agreed.

"Two more months, though," he said. "Can you believe it? It'll be my first time off."

Off the island. Away from By-the-Sea. Another small contingent of freshly graduated By-the-Sea teenagers stepping onto the ferry and leaving home for the first time in their entire lives.

It actually wasn't as weird as it sounded. Most kids didn't leave until college. Although small, the island had everything you might need: a four-lane bowling alley; a high school, middle school, and grade school; and one grocery store (that admittedly did sometimes run out of food, but we had learned to stock up and also cultivate little gardens).

"It doesn't seem possible," I answered finally. And it didn't. In that moment, the entire world was just By-the-Sea, just the Beach, just my sister dancing in the ice-cold water.

"I know what you mean," Colin agreed. "Like we've

been waiting our whole lives and now it's just around the corner." He knocked his knee into mine. "All right, we should at least get our feet wet."

So we waded out up to our ankles in the water, and I tried to decide what laughing, soaking-wet shape was my sister, or Vira, or anyone.

Mary found me quickly enough, running past me like a bullet to get to her dress on the blanket. She pulled it over her head and then came back to where I was standing.

"Every year," she said. "Every year I forget a towel. Hi, Colin."

"Hi, Mary," he said.

One by one our peers emerged from the water, running back to wherever they'd stashed their clothes, wrapping themselves in blankets and towels if they'd been smart enough to think ahead.

Colin wandered away, and Mary and I picked our way back to the blanket and settled around it in a lazy circle. Shelby lay down in the middle, looking up at the stars.

Abigail packed a fresh bowl and passed it around our small group. I took only one very small hit, because Abigail's stuff was homegrown and strong and I was a lightweight and didn't want to get lost on the way home. Mary skipped it altogether, probably because the last time she'd smoked weed she'd drifted lazily upward and almost decapitated herself on a ceiling fan. "This is nice," Shelby said, prone to the sentimental when she'd had a little of Abigail's stash.

"This is like the first night of the rest of our lives."

"That's exactly what I said!" Mary said.

"Every night is the first night of the rest of our lives," Vira retorted.

"That's exactly what *I* said," I said, and then I hugged Vira because she was the most perfect princess in the world.

Oh shit. See? That was the weed.

After a long stretch of quiet, I nudged Mary and asked, "Ready? You've danced *and* swum naked. Swimming wasn't even part of the deal."

"Yeah, yeah, I'm ready. Has anybody seen my shoes?"

Someone tossed them to her, and after a lot of hugging (dancing naked really endears you to people, and we were a huggy group anyway), Mary and I set off back up the Beach, back toward Bottle Hill and Fernweh Inn and our attic home and our nice warm beds.

And that was how it was: the start of every summer since Mary and I'd been old enough to figure out how to sneak out of the inn. The revelry and singing would grow louder and louder. Eventually the rest of the party (sans Mary and me, who would already be safely home) would be broken up by the sheriff or deputy, a lackluster police involvement that was more out of duty than any real passion for the laws we were breaking. (Beaches closed at dusk; underage drinking; lack of proper permits for a bonfire; indecent exposure.) We would not get enough sleep. The birdheads would arrive tomorrow, dozens of them, filling up every corner of the inn. They would bring us presents, the ones who'd known us since we were kids. They would hug us and tuck postcards and five-dollar bills into our pockets. We would get no damn rest or privacy for the next two months: the season of Annabella. Arriving like clockwork. All the fuss in the world over a silly little bird—who, I admit, I loved more than any of the birdheads, more than any of the islanders, because I felt somehow that she belonged to me, to all the Fernweh women, in a way, but especially to me.

The moon drifted in and out of existence. My sister took my hand and squeezed, and I felt that squeeze on my fingers and somehow on my heart as the singing drifted across the sand to reach us:

On By-the-Sea, you and me will be forever young . . .

Oh, By-the-Sea, island of Fernwehs and everything I had ever known and loved. How I would miss you—every part of you—but especially the smell, always the smell: of salt, of brine, of water, of spells, of potions, of feathers, and of what it would mean to leave it all in just two months.

CHECK-IN

Mary and I were born in a rainstorm that flooded the streets and overwhelmed the sewers and drowned the beaches of By-the-Sea and turned everything wet and gray for seven days.

I've heard this story many times, enough times that it feels like I actually remember it.

My mother was in the kitchen, cutting wedges of lime to squeeze into the virgin margaritas she'd been addicted to during her pregnancy. She felt off—nothing enormous, just a tiny headache, a sliver of fatigue, a faint unease in her abdomen.

She made her drink and took it onto the front porch and sat down in a wicker rocking chair and sipped and rocked and sipped and rocked.

Then one of the housekeepers saw her and said, "Mrs. Fernweh, you don't look so hot. I think you may be about to have a couple babies."

"I had just figured that out myself," my mother said, and raised her glass in a toast.

She hadn't wanted to rush her drink.

My father worked as a fisherman; my mother sent word down to the docks that the babies were coming, and then she got into her pickup truck and drove herself to the small hospital, so small it wasn't even named, so small there were only five parking spaces and four were free. She parked and went inside and filled out some forms and walked herself down to the birthing room, which was also the emergency room and the surgery room and the recovery room and, on Friday nights, the movie room.

I came first, a full five hours before my sister. I came out easily, noisily, red-faced and screaming, hardly half an hour after my mother had lain down.

I came out, and then the rains started, and then the doctor told my mother, *Hold off on pushing again, at least for a while, this second one seems to be a little stubborn.*

"Has anybody heard from my husband?" my mother asked, smiling down at me, wrapped in that generic hospital baby blanket that not even By-the-Sea's small hospital was lacking.

Outside, the skies had unzipped themselves and the rain fell so thickly that all you could see were lines of gray against gray.

But nobody had heard from my father.

"The rain is heavy; it should drive the boats in," the nurse, Emery Grace, said. "He'll be here soon, maybe even in time for number two."

My mom patted her stomach gingerly. "This one's called Mary." She touched my forehead. "This one's Georgina."

"Georgina, that's beautiful."

"It's a family name. Has somebody called the docks?"

Emery shook her head sadly. "It's the phone lines, Penny. The storm's knocked them all down."

"Can I get up? If it's going to be a while?"

"You're really not supposed to."

"I just want to sit by the window," my mother said.

So Emery raised the back of my mom's hospital bed and undid the brakes and rolled the whole thing over to the window, with me still wrapped in that blanket, trying to figure out how to nurse.

When I'd had enough milk, my mother turned me around and tucked my head under her chin, and we watched the rain come down while we waited for my sister, while we waited for my father.

But only one of them would ever show up.

Nobody ever saw my father again. His boat went down in the storm; the small crew was lost.

Now I think of him whenever it rains. And sometimes—though I know it's impossible—it rains whenever I think of him.

That was what I was dreaming about—the storm, the

flooded island, my mother with her two small babies in a rowboat—when Mary threw herself on my bed the morning after the bonfire, so early that the room was still dark. My head pounded—half from the cinnamon whiskey, half from the lack of sleep. I groaned and tried to hit her.

"You overslept, and Mom is pi-i-issed," Mary sang, catching my hand and forcing something into it. I cracked an eyelid: a banana muffin. I took a bite and chewed.

"My alarm's set," I mumbled through muffin.

"Yeah, I checked, and you actually set it for six *tonight*, which is very cute wishful thinking on your part. It's almost seven now, and I've been ironing napkins for an hour."

I grabbed Mary's arm with my free hand and pulled myself up to a sitting position. The room tilted dangerously. She held a mug of steaming coffee out to me, and I took it, gulping gratefully, not even caring about the inevitable mouth blisters I was giving myself. That little piece of skin right behind my top teeth was already shriveling up.

"Did you sleep well? I slept really well," Mary said, stretching her arms over her head luxuriantly.

"Check-in isn't till *noon*," I whined.

"Yes, well, those napkins aren't going to iron themselves, my friend." Mary hopped to her feet. "Take a shower, and I'll tell Mom you'll be down soon. I can buy you twenty minutes, maybe."

"Thirty?"

"The wishful thinking again! I wish I could be as

positive as you, Georgie, I really do. And so early in the morning!"

She left me, thankfully, alone. I propped my pillow up behind me and leaned back against the bed so I could finish eating my muffin. Five hours until check-in and I needed about forty-seven showers and twelve more muffins. And another half-dozen cups of coffee too. I finished what I had, shoved the remaining bit of muffin in my mouth, and stumbled down the hall to the bathroom.

It was just us up here: my bedroom, Mary's bedroom, our bathroom, and a room of storage stuffed so full of boxes you couldn't take more than two steps into it. The Fernweh Inn had four floors, including this one, and for ten months of the year they sat abandoned. By-the-Sea had a short tourist season, but it was also a busy one. We would make enough in two months to get by until next summer.

In the bathroom I got naked and waited for the water to heat up, jumping from foot to foot to help myself wake up. When it was hot enough, I stepped into the shower and stood directly under the stream, letting the water hit me in my face until I was sure that all the salt and sand from the night before was washed off my skin (although it would never be all washed off, not really). I felt better afterward, albeit marginally. I toweled off and then made my way back to my bedroom to get dressed.

I took my coffee cup downstairs to the kitchen for a refill. Aggie, Mom's best friend and the official cook of the Fernweh Inn, was prepping that day's dinner in the kitchen. When she saw me, she burst out laughing. Aggie's laugh was like a bus horn, loud and sharp. She was a tall woman who always wore a scarf wrapped around her long gray hair. She was like a second mother to me, especially during the summer months, when she practically lived at the inn. She laughed again now at the sight of me; Aggie was always either laughing or cooking, and often both at the same time.

"Georgina, you look like something the cat dragged in," she said. I poured more coffee and yawned.

"It was the solstice last night. I didn't want to go. Mary made me."

"Ah, it's tradition. You'll feel fine after you wake up a little. Do you want an omelet?"

"I had a muffin."

"That's a new recipe; you like 'em?"

"Really good. Thanks, Aggie."

"Well, they won't cure a hangover, but they might help a little."

"I sure hope you didn't say 'hangover' in reference to my daughter, who is, last I checked, underage," my mom said, bustling into the kitchen in her usual flurry of motion. She wore an ankle-length dress the color of midnight. *Which is not exactly my cup of tea, but adds to the aesthetic. Old inn, old island, old scary dress, you get it*, she'd once said. "Georgina, you're late," she added.

"I'm sorry. I set my alarm wrong."

"Well, I need you on silverware duty for now, okay? Wash and polish, honey, that stuff hasn't been touched since last August." She pointed to the sink, next to which was a massive pile of the good silver forks and spoons and knives. I spent five seconds of freedom staring at the pile, unmoving, and then I went and filled the sink with water.

It took ages to wash the endless pile of silverware (endless largely in part because Mom kept finding more of it and bringing it over to me with an evil, joyous smirk plastered on her face), and when I was done I set up a station in the dining room where I could polish and shine.

For not the first time in my life as a Fernweh woman, I wished magic was more like it was in the movies. On TV, people snapped their fingers and piles of silverware obligingly sprang to life and washed themselves. On By-the-Sea, not so much.

Sure, we all had our specialties (except me, who had none): My mother could make any potion she set her mind to. My great-grandmother Roberta had controlled fire; her mother before her could walk on water and breathe underneath it. My sister, with absolutely no practice or seemingly much interest at all, had mastered the act of jumping out her bedroom window, and here I was, stuck washing silver by hand.

It wasn't that I hadn't *tried* to make my powers come. I had. Especially when I was younger.

I used to put myself in the weirdest situations, just to see if anything would happen.

I'd stuck my head in the full bathtub and taken a tentative breath.

I'd placed my hand over an open flame to see if it maybe wouldn't hurt, if maybe fire was my thing.

I'd tried to talk to animals.

I'd tried a hundred things over the years, and then I'd given up, resigning myself to the fact that it would either happen or it wouldn't, and I probably had no say either way.

It was only just getting light outside when I started polishing; I was on my fourth cup of coffee (to be fair, Aggie's coffee was notoriously weak), and I had only caught glimpses of my sister as she jumped from one task to another, never in one place for very long, always with an extreme eye roll for me as Mom followed closely behind her, barking instructions. I had just managed to find a way to fall half-asleep while still mechanically polishing forks when I finished. Almost immediately, my mother was upon me with the next thing I had to do.

Hours later—*years* later—I was somehow done washing and polishing the silverware, ironing and hanging a hundred million curtains, dusting off the room keys (seriously), sweeping the front porch, beating out the cushions on the wicker furniture on said porch, and making sure Fernweh Inn's twelve grandfather clocks were all wound and set to the correct time. By then it was eleven-thirty and time for a quick lunch before the guests started arriving.

I'd checked the register earlier; of the inn's sixteen rooms (floors two and three held the guest rooms, eight apiece), I knew all but six of today's arrivals. That was to be expected: our crowd was mostly repeat birdheads, mixed in with a few random tourists who usually stayed a weekend or a week and left disappointed and confused about our priorities. The birdheads would be here until August. You'd be surprised at how easily these birdheads afforded my mother's not-shy room rates. I knew one guy—Tank Smith—who routinely sold photos of Annabella's Woodpecker to the *Geographic Times* for more money than most people make in a year. He spent the rest of the year doing God knows what, came to By-the-Sea for two months, snapped a picture, and made a cool hundred Gs.

I met Aggie, Mom, and Mary in the kitchen for lunch. Mom handed me a gray, curiously smoking drink. I looked into the glass skeptically. It smelled like a match the moment you blow out the flame. Acidic and bitter and hot.

"It will make you feel better," she said, winking. The wink meant that the stuff in my hand wasn't your run-of-the-mill smoothie.

Although people on the island didn't go around openly acknowledging the general magicness of my family, it was common knowledge that if you wanted something done, Penelope Fernweh could sometimes, with the right greasing of the wheels, do it for you. You didn't ask questions. You didn't make assumptions. You'd just slip her a little cash for her trouble and let her do her thing: bury this or that under a full moon, throw some shady ingredients into a big copper pot (you wouldn't call it a cauldron, obviously), boil a frog alive and drink the marrow from its bones (just kidding; she never hurt animals). And then you'd sit back and wait. In this case, you'd wait for it to cure your hangover.

"Wait—why wouldn't you have given this to me at *seven in the morning*?" I whined.

"I thought I should make you suffer a little. You *did* drink the rest of my good cinnamon whiskey. Do you know how long I'd been infusing that?"

I was going to argue with her, clarify that it had actually been Mary who'd stolen the whiskey, but I decided against it. She who giveth could easily taketh away, and besides, I was used to being blamed for the trouble my sister got herself into. It was just sort of the way of the world. Mary did something rash; I inevitably helped her wiggle out of trouble.

I sipped at the smoothie and instantly felt better. *Magic*, I mouthed at Mary, who rolled her eyes and held out her hand for a taste.

"Finally, the sun!" Aggie exclaimed, peering out the window. "It's been so gloomy all morning."

"You couldn't have added some strawberries to this, Ma?" Mary said, pretending to gag. "It tastes awful."

"The beggars and the choosers," Mom said.

Aggie dished out quiche to the table; I was just finishing my second piece when the door to the kitchen opened and Peter Elmhurst, bellboy/groundskeeper/jack-of-all-trades, poked his head in.

"Ms. Fernweh," he said, "the first guests are arriving."

Aggie held up a Bloody Mary I hadn't even noticed she was drinking. (If Aggie's coffee was weak, her Bloody Marys were the opposite.) "To another season," she said brightly.

"To Annabella," Mom added. "May this finally be her year."

She meant the eggs. Poor Annabella, perpetually childless. She laid eggs every summer, but they never hatched, no matter how diligently she tended to them. It was a big ornithological mystery, the will-she/won't-she back-and-forth and the letdown when, one August morning, inevitably, she would be gone, and the eggs would remain behind, useless and cold. (Every year they were carefully collected and brought back to the mainland and autopsied. Every year they could find nothing obvious pointing to why they hadn't survived incubation.)

We Fernwehs knew, of course, that Annabella wasn't strictly your average bird, and that her eggs probably weren't hatching because of that.

"To Annabella," I echoed, raising my glass.

And, fully embracing our long-held status as the biggest

weirdos this side of the mainland, we toasted to a little bird and her fertility problems: Aggie and Mom with Bloody Marys, Mary and me with a sip of legit magic potion.

It had turned out to be a beautiful day. By-the-Sea weather had always been a little unpredictable (the rainstorms of our birth come to mind), but it had only seemed to get worse lately: it would be summer and warm one minute, rainy and miserable the next, blizzard conditions the day after that. And the island paid no attention at all to conventional seasons. It had once snowed in July (the birdheads built a little lean-to around Annabella's chosen tree). It had once been a blazing 110 degrees in January (we all went to the Beach and decided not to question things). By now we were all used to it. It wasn't unusual for the birdheads to show up with both swimming trunks and skis packed into their enormous traveling trunks.

I watched the first few of them walking up the front path now, all familiar faces: Liesel Channing and Hep Shackman, Henrietta Lee behind him followed by Tank Smith, the photographer. I'd seen these people every summer since I was born, and weird as they were, they were almost like family.

Liesel reached me first. She wore pale-purple chinos with a pale-purple oxford shirt and pale-purple sneakers. And pale-purple-rimmed glasses. The only thing on her person that was not purple (luggage: purple; hair tie: purple) was her dutiful birdcat (like a birddog, but an exceptionally grumpy orange Maine coon named Horace, complete with heart-shaped birthmark on its forehead). She gasped when she finally made it up the porch steps. "It cannot be, it is *impossible*! You're a woman now! Where has my little Georgina gone to!"

"Liesel, it's so nice to see you!" I said, giving her a hug. By then the others had reached us (Hep, Henrietta, and Tank were significantly older than Liesel and had slowed down considerably over the years), and I made sure to hug and kiss every one of them. I was the front porch welcoming committee; Mary was just inside the front doors. The lucky thing was that there was only one taxi on By-the-Sea (driven by Seymore Stanners, Shelby's dad, complete with a little flatbed wagon he pulled behind it for all the luggage), and so the arrivals would be limited to groups of four. Small doses of birdheads were better.

Once this group disappeared inside I collapsed on a wicker armchair and closed my eyes, enjoying the sunshine and the warmth of the day.

I didn't have much time to myself, though. Half a minute later I heard a small cough and opened my eyes to see Peter Elmhurst standing uncomfortably close to me, smelling of firewood and smoke.

"Hi, Peter."

"Hi, Georgie," he said, then stopped.

Peter lived down the road, on a farm near the cemetery.

We'd all grown up together and used to be closer as kids, but we'd sort of drifted apart over the years. I blamed that on him—he'd been tragically in love with my sister since we were seven, and he really didn't know how to take *no thanks* for an answer.

"I brought the firewood," Peter said. "In case your mom asks. It's already out back."

"I'll tell her." He shuffled his feet but didn't make a move to leave. "Anything else?"

"I was just wondering if I could talk to you for a second?"

I already knew what was coming; if I had a dollar for every boy on this island that asked me why my sister hadn't fallen madly in love with him, I'd have enough for a ticket to the mainland. And first month's rent on a new apartment. And a brand-new car. And so on.

"Sure, Peter. What's going on?"

"I'm sorry if this is inappropriate. I know technically we work together, you know? I was actually just curious if maybe your sister had mentioned . . . Well, I wrote her a letter. And she hasn't said anything. So I'm sort of worried now that maybe I forgot a stamp? Or maybe I got the address wrong? One Bottle Hill Lane, right?"

The island was so small that you honestly didn't need addresses. If I wrote "Elvira Montgomery" on an envelope, with nothing else but a lipstick kiss for directions, it would reach her in two hours. Our postman, Albert Craws, was very good. And he was also very generous; I never used stamps. I sometimes wrote him nice things where a stamp should go—*Hope you're well, Albert! Don't work too hard, Albert!*—but I had never once actually paid to send a letter. Peter could have messed up every single step of mailing that letter to my sister and it still would have gotten here. Which meant of course she'd received it, of course she'd showed it to me, and of course she had no intention of writing him back.

"I don't think she mentioned anything about a letter," I said, hating to lie to him, hating my sister for making it necessary for me to lie to him, hating my sister for always managing to drag me into her problems. "You know my mom. She's so absentminded, she probably checked the mail and ended up burying the letter in her rose garden."

My mother was anything but absentminded, but it seemed like a good excuse; she did occasionally bury non-rose things in the rose garden.

I couldn't tell if Peter bought it. His face flushed a quick red, and he took a visible breath. Then in a small, even voice he said, "I just think if someone takes the time to write you a letter, you should respond to them."

"Maybe you should write another one and hand deliver it?"

Even my sister would have a hard time pretending she hadn't gotten a hand-delivered letter.

"Sure," Peter said, shrugging, relaxing, smiling a little.

"Yeah, I could do that. Thanks, Georgina. I guess I'll see you around."

He disappeared around the back of the house.

Mary joined me a second later, like she'd been staring out the window, waiting for him to leave.

"Why does it feel like I'm always apologizing for you?" I asked her. She sat on the arm of the chair I was in and played with my hair. We both had long hair, all the way down our backs, but that was mostly because the island's one hairdresser, Shirley Braves, was impossible to track down and also, inexplicably, hated cutting hair.

"I never asked you to lie for me. And I've never promised Peter anything," Mary countered.

"So if you don't like him, you need to cut him loose. Once and for all. Snip, snip, snip."

"You're being a real nosy Rosey, you know that?" she said, getting off the arm of the chair, wheeling around to face me. "I can hang out with whoever the fuck I want *and* I can fuck whoever I want to hang out with. . . ." She squinted, as if trying to figure out if that made sense.

"Truce. It's too hot to fight," I said.

"Yeah, what's up with that?" she asked, instantly distracted. "I thought I saw snow flurries this morning, but it's beautiful now. Oh, great. Another taxi. I'll see you later."

She went back inside.

It was like that all day, taxi after taxi bringing birdhead after birdhead to the inn.

The light was starting to change by the time my mom came out onto the front porch. "We're only waiting for a few more guests," she said. "Great turnout this year, huh? How are you feeling, Georgie?"

"I'm fine," I said. Above us, a cloud hid the sun and I shivered.

"That's probably the last of them right now," Mom said, pointing down the drive at Seymore's cab just turning into view. She put her hand on my shoulder. "You can take a nap before dinner, Georgina. Put on a happy face for now, okay?"

I smiled as big and fake as I could. She rolled her eyes and went back inside. Mary caught the door and slipped out onto the porch before it closed.

"The lobby is filled with birdheads," she whined. Then, seeing the taxi: "Oh thank God, is that the last of them?"

"Who are we missing? Nobody we know, right?"

"I looked at the register; these are newbs. A man and a woman. Two twin beds. So like, unhappily married, I'm guessing."

"Or friends."

"Right, because you take so many island vacations with your platonic male friends?"

Mary was in one of her moods, when everything you said became fair game for a fight. She was probably just as tired as I was. I looked down at her feet: the soles of her shoes were a solid half inch above the porch. I yanked her

down, and she mumbled an apology but then visibly bright-
ened. I followed her gaze down to the driveway, where our
last guests were just emerging from Seymore's car.

Where our last, very young and attractive guests were
just emerging from Seymore's car.

"Oh," I said.

"Oh shi-i-it," Mary whispered. "What time is it,
Georgie?"

"I'm not saying."

"Georgieeeee."

"I'm not saying it."

"Georgie, what time is it?"

"Cute o'clock," I relented. "It's cute o'clock, okay, you
psychopath."

I stepped off the porch, waiting on the last step as
Seymore helped our very young and attractive guests with
their luggage. This was no married couple. The guy looked
like he was a few years older than me—twenty-three or
twenty-four—and the girl seemed about my age.

Suddenly Mary's mouth was right next to my ear.
"There's one for each of us," she hissed, and when I turned
around to smack her she leapt gracefully out of my reach.
Winking, she retreated into the inn.

I walked closer to the car. The guy was paying Seymore, thanking him, laughing about something. The girl
was blank-faced, unreadable, looking past me and up at the
inn. She slid her red-framed sunglasses up onto her head

and finally noticed me, holding my gaze for a long time, for as long as it took the guy to finish paying. When her traveling partner tapped her on the shoulder and handed her a suitcase, she took it without complaint and shifted her focus from me to him. An unkind sort of look. A look of annoyance. If they *were* married, it was definitely not a happy union.

I made the conscious shift from normal-Georgina to working-Georgina, checked that my smile was as genuine as possible, and met them on the driveway.

"Hi, there! Welcome to Fernweh Inn. Is this your first time on By-the-Sea?"

"It is!" the guy said, dropping one of his bags so he could shake my hand. "I'm Harrison Lowry. This is Prudence."

"Prue," she corrected, extending her hand and giving a weak, but not unkind, smile. Then Harrison reached over to tousle her hair, and her eyes rolled back so far in her head that I knew instantly: oh, duh. Brother and sister.

"I haven't been able to get a signal since we left the mainland," Harrison said, holding up his phone. "Is that normal?"

"Welcome to By-the-Sea," I said, sweeping my hand over the island. "That's just kind of how it is."

He smiled and shrugged a bit. "Well, I guess that can't be helped."

Harrison was cute, I had to give him that. He was tall and his hair was a messy brown and his eyes were bright and his smile was genuine. He wore long pants and actual suspenders with a short-sleeved button-up shirt. He had that nerdy-but-I'm-running-with-it thing. I wouldn't have expected him to be a birdhead, but the evidence was there: oversized leather camera bag, small binoculars already slung around his neck, dingy suitcase practically covered in antique bird patches.

Prue was more of a mystery. She wore high-waisted jean shorts that looked vintage, a blue-and-white-striped T-shirt that looked vintage and French, and faded red lipstick that just looked really, really good. Her hair was a darker brown than her brother's and hit just above her shoulders. They looked alike in a vague sort of way, just how two people who've lived together their whole lives inevitably start to blend a little around the edges.

"Where are you visiting from?" I asked.

"Just flat dab in the middle of the mainland," Harrison said, adding "kind of person who says flat dab" to my short list of things I knew about him.

"Oh, well, that's nice you're able to travel together. Are you two . . ."

"Brother and sister," Harrison finished, confirming my suspicions.

"Georgina! I'm sure our guests want to get inside and see their rooms," Mary said, bounding up next to me. I hadn't even heard the front door open. She was sneaky, my sister. She linked her arm through mine, and her smile was so bright I could feel the heat coming off her face. "I'm Mary," she continued, detaching herself from me and sticking a hand out to Harrison, then Prue.

"Harrison," he said. "My sister, Prudence."

"Perfect," Mary purred (there really isn't a more accurate word for it). "I'll get you guys all settled into your room. It's one of our nicest ones; excellent view of the sea."

Wishful thinking, maybe, but I almost swore that Prue met my eye for just the tiniest fraction of a second and smiled just the tiniest fraction of a smile.

There was a big dinner that night to celebrate the birdheads' arrival (and the, like, four inn guests who weren't birdheads but who *were* very confused and kept looking around like they had gotten off at the wrong island). Aggie went all out in the way she always did the first night of the season. We had it in the backyard and practically the entire population of By-the-Sea showed up.

Mary and I ate at a table with Vira, Abigail, Eloise, and Shelby. We were exactly two tables away from Harrison and Prue, and my sister's eyes were trained on the former in a *not-at-all-serial-killer way, thankyouverymuch, Georgina, and also mind your own damn business.*

"You *are* my business," I said. "We're twins, so people automatically lump us together. When you do asinine things, they just naturally get associated with me."

"Luckily for you I've never done an asinine thing in my

life," she said, and winked, because not even Mary could say that with a straight face. Then, more serious, settling back in her chair and using a garlic breadstick as a pointer, she said, "Do you think he's cute?"

I grabbed the breadstick from her before anybody saw the direction in which she was waggling it. "He's a *guest*," I said.

"What are you, the one-man human resource department of the Fernweh Inn?" She plucked the breadstick out of my hand and threw it across the table. "Yo, Shelbs. Hot or not?" She jerked her finger in Harrison's direction.

Shelby, picking up the breadstick from where it had ricocheted off her forehead, took a thoughtful bite and considered. "Hot," she decided after a moment. "Really hot. He's not a birdhead, is he?"

I nodded. "He's new."

"And the girl?" Abigail asked. All conversation at the table had ceased, and now seven eager pairs of eyes were staring openly at the Lowrys' table.

"Sister," Mary said.

"The girl's pretty too," Eloise said, in her usual thoughtful manner. "What's her name?"

"Prudence," Mary said.

"Prue," I corrected, perhaps a bit too quickly.

"Ohhh," Vira said, nodding.

"What oh? Oh what?" I asked.

"Nothing," she replied quickly, filling her mouth with

mashed potatoes so she wouldn't have to answer.

"Ohhh," Shelby echoed. She nodded appreciatively. "Yeah, that makes sense. She's definitely your type. She looks like she belongs on a picnic blanket under the Eiffel Tower, eating a baguette or something."

"You guys are being assholes," I said.

"*You're* being a hypocrite," Mary countered, and stole a carrot from my plate.

Eloise, angel that she was, changed the subject then to something no one could resist gossiping about for the rest of dinner: was Joel Howard, owner and proprietor of Joel's Diner, actually going to do as he'd been threatening for years and stop having free fries on Friday?

"But it's called *Free Fries Friday*," Abigail said, horrified, and they were off, a mile a minute about how Joel was on pretty thin ice with all of them, if the rumors were true.

"Thanks for changing the subject," I said to Eloise later, when the dinner was over and Aggie and Peter were setting up the dessert table.

"Honestly, they're too nosy sometimes," she replied.

"I haven't really liked anyone since Verity," I said. "I think my sister is just thrilled at the prospect. Especially if she wants to go after a guest. Strength in numbers, I guess."

"You don't have to explain yourself to me," Eloise insisted. "It's a small island. I think it's important to keep some sort of privacy."

I waited until the guests had had the first pickings of the

dessert table and then grabbed a plate for myself. Aggie's cinnamon cheesecake was unreal and aside from that she'd made four different kinds of brownies, twelve types of cookies, an assortment of mini pies, and a cake made as the exact replica of the inn. I took a little bit of everything.

It was cooler out now, but Peter had gotten the fire pit going, and the fire caught on the wind and blew warm air all over the yard. I brought my plate over to one of the benches that dotted the lawn, looking out over the southern tip of the island and the dark ocean beyond. I'd been avoiding Mary and the others pretty deftly so was both annoyed and discouraged when I heard footsteps behind me—and then immediately terrified and thrilled when Prue asked if she could sit with me.

"Yes! I mean, sure. I mean, if you want to," I said, sliding over, hating myself for how hard words could be.

"If you don't mind," she said. She sat down and showed me some fluorescent-colored liquid in a paper cup. "Do you know what this is? It was in that enormous, car-sized bowl," she said.

"Ah, that's Albert's Postal Punch. Be careful with it; it's sort of disgusting and also unrealistically strong."

"Unrealistically strong, I like that," she said, smiling. The moon was out and high in the sky, and that, coupled with the lights from the lanterns that were scattered around the lawn, made Prue look ethereal, almost too pretty to focus on. Then she took a sip of punch and immediately spit it out in an impressive arc onto the grass, and I couldn't help it, I burst out laughing, just barely managing not to snort.

"God, what *is* that?" she said, coughing.

"I warned you."

"I've learned my lesson; I'll listen to you from now on." She spit again, then poured the rest of the punch onto the grass. I offered her my dessert plate.

"To get the taste out of your mouth."

"This is a liberal spread you have here," she said.

"I haven't had Aggie's cooking since last August, so I'm just remembering how good it is."

Prue picked a peanut butter brownie off the plate and took a big bite. "Oh wow," she said through a mouthful of chocolate. "Oh geez."

"I know, right?" I set the plate on the bench between us. "Be my guest."

"Technically, I *am* your guest," she said, swallowing. "You live here, right? At the inn?"

"Since we were born."

"Oh, yeah. Mary . . . she's your twin, right?"

"In everything but looks and personality."

"Yeah, you don't look alike. Is it cool, living here? It's kind of . . ."

"Creepy?"

"No, I like the inn. I mean the island. Does it ever seem . . . small?"

Did it ever seem small, this island I had spent every minute of my waking life on, this island I knew like I knew my own body, this island where every tree was named and everyone knew each other and every person played some intimate, vital role in making sure it functioned smoothly, day after day after day until the day I left, until the day we all would leave, to seek our fortunes elsewhere.

"Do you know how the Amish leave home and spend a year just sort of doing whatever they've always wanted to do?" I asked.

"Rumspringa," she responded.

"And you know how almost all of them return home after that and never leave again? That's kind of like this island."

"Heavy."

"Yeah. But that's how it is everywhere, right? It's hard to leave the place you grew up."

"I wouldn't really know; we've always traveled around a lot. My father's an archaeologist and my mother's a linguistic anthropologist. Harrison and I were homeschooled, dragged all over the place. Our parents have settled down now, retired, but I still feel kind of . . . untethered."

"How did you end up here?"

"My brother. He's in graduate school for ornithology; this is part of his research. It was either tagging along with him, official sister-cum-lab-assistant, or stay with my parents until college. They're great, don't get me wrong, but

I'm used to traveling. So I picked the lesser of two familial evils, and here I am." She paused, took a bite of cookie. "It's kind of charming, this island. I hope that didn't come across like I didn't like it."

"Oh, no. It *is* small. I think I'm just used to it."

Behind us the birdheads were loud and rambunctious, stretching their legs after a full year of doing whatever they did when they weren't looking for Annabella.

As if she could read my mind, Prue asked, "So what's the deal with the bird? My brother wouldn't stop talking about it for the entire trip over here, but honestly, I get a little sick on boats, so I think I missed most of it. She only shows up during the summer, right? Where does she go for the rest of the year?"

Where did Annabella go? Somewhere far, far away, if she knew what was good for her. Somewhere where the rumspringa never ended. Somewhere where she didn't have to deal with birdheads documenting her every turn, photographing every tiny movement of her head, singing songs to her at night before they left her to get some sleep. Somewhere where she didn't have to worry about eggs that didn't hatch and summers that kept feeling shorter and shorter. Somewhere where you couldn't smell the ocean, somewhere where the ocean was the faintest memory. A rumor heard from a friend of a friend of a friend. Somewhere where the color blue did not exist.

"Georgina?" Prue asked.

"Sorry. What was the question?"

"Forget the question," she said with a wave of her hand. She forked a bite of Fernweh Inn–shaped cake and handed it to me. "Questions later. Cake now."

I took the fork obediently.

The sound of crashing waves—never really absent on By-the-Sea but only sometimes, for a few minutes, faded enough into the background that you didn't really notice them—swelled up and momentarily overwhelmed the night. I ate the cake. Prue took another cookie.

Mary could fly. I wished I could stop time.

"I saw you talking to that girl," Mary said later in the bathroom we shared, a long piece of floss woven through her fingers. It was past midnight, and it felt like I'd been up for a hundred years. I sat on the edge of the claw-foot bathtub and waited my turn at the sink.

"Prue. She seems nice."

"You li-i-i-ike her," Mary said. She lifted herself onto the vanity and sat facing me, not flossing with the floss, just playing with it.

"I only just met her."

"You can like people you just met. You can even like people you haven't even met yet. You can even like people—"

"Did you talk to her brother?"

"What, am I allowed? You told me he was a guest.

Which, by the way, I thought was pretty rich since you flirted with Prue all night."

"It was twenty minutes, it wasn't all night, and I've come to accept the inevitability of you sleeping with Harrison this summer. Despite the fact that he's a birdhead, which sort of goes against all laws of logic."

"I dunno, his birdheadedness just somehow adds to his charm," she said, winking. "Is Prue nice?"

"She seems nice."

"How come she's here? She's not a birdhead too, is she? She doesn't seem like a birdhead."

"She's just tagging along with her brother."

"Poor girl. She probably has no friends."

"You're an asshole."

"No judgment! Who needs friends?" She hopped off the vanity, threw the floss in the trash, and spread a line of toothpaste on her brush.

"You have friends, Mary."

"I have you, Georgie. I don't need anybody else."

"Well, you won't have me at college, so you'll have to make some new friends."

"Ugh. That sounds exhausting. They should assign you friends like they assign you a roommate. By the way, have you gotten yours yet? I'm with someone named Mildred Miller. That's a truly unfortunate name. I hope she's, like, unreal hot. For her sake, you know."

"I wouldn't lead with that in your introductions."

"God, you think I'm such a jerk," she said, rolling her eyes and brushing her teeth.

"I don't think you're a jerk."

Mary spit, rinsed, and turned to look at me again. "Are you nervous?" she asked, suddenly serious.

I knew exactly what she was talking about, of course, and it wasn't college. But I had no desire to get into it at the current moment. I gave a noncommittal shrug and pushed her out of the way so I could wash my face.

"I mean, I'd be nervous. If I were you. I'd be just a little nervous," she continued, moving to the toilet, sitting down on the closed lid, and crossing her legs. "I'm not saying *you* should be nervous, but *I* would be nervous."

"Can you shut up?"

"Do you not want to talk about it?"

"The queen of deduction."

"Our birthday is two months away."

"Thank you, Mary, I remembered."

"And you still haven't shown any signs of—"

"Grandma Berry was seventeen years and three hundred and sixty-four days old before she showed any signs of—"

"Lower your voice! Do you want to wake a birdhead?"

"Grandma Berry," I repeated, hissing, "did not show any signs of magic until the day before her eighteenth birthday."

"And I bet *she* was nervous," Mary said thoughtfully. I

wanted to grab the nearest hairbrush and beat her over the head with it, but I settled for brushing my teeth so hard my gums turned bright red.

When I finished, Mary was staring intently at me, her forehead knitted up in lines.

"But what about the twin thing?" she asked quietly.

"What twin thing?" I asked, although I knew exactly what she was talking about, of course I did.

"The first Georgina. She never got powers, but her sister Annabella did. Her twin. There haven't been twins in our family since."

"Our great-great-aunt's daughter never got powers either, and she was an only child. It's not like I'll *die*, Mary, I'll just go on living like every other person in the history of the world who isn't in our family. Being able to float three inches off the ground isn't the fucking miracle you make it out to be."

Mary's shoulders lowered a fraction of an inch, the only sign to indicate that I'd struck a nerve.

"I'm sorry," she said. "I shouldn't have brought it up again."

"Look, it's okay. Of course I keep thinking about it. Of course I'm nervous, or . . . not nervous, really, but just . . . curious. But I do mean that; it's not the end of the world if I'm not a . . ."

We didn't say the word out loud—that little word assigned to the women in our family—there was rarely a need. Mary reached her hand out and squeezed my fingers, squeezed every knuckle.

"I'm tired," she said.

"A long day of annoying me, I don't blame you," I said, but softly, so she'd know I was joking. She got up and hugged me quickly, then slipped out of the bathroom. I shut the door and took her place on the toilet, next to the open window. And fuck, although I didn't want to, although I really didn't want to, I started crying.

Outside, a massive crack of thunder and the unmistakable patter of rain.

Like a sign from the heavens. We feel you, girl. We got your back. We'll like you no matter if you get your powers or not. We could really care less.

Me too, Sky. I could care less too.

DAYS LATE

Annabella didn't show up the next day or the day after that. I was busy at the inn, my mother constantly had me shuffling between housekeeping duties, cooking duties, concierge duties (those were the best, our four non-birdhead guests asked easy questions and had seemed to accept that their weeklong summer vacation was being shared with a bunch of weirdo bird enthusiasts).

Wherever Annabella was, she was making the birdheads antsy, even though her absence wasn't that unheard of. Yeah, she *usually* showed up promptly on the day after the summer solstice, but she was also just a bird. You couldn't count on birds.

"The record lateness is one week," Lucille Arden said at breakfast, three days since the solstice. Lucille was the youngest birdhead—besides Harrison now—and celebrating her tenth summer on the island. She accepted a muffin from Aggie, who was walking around with a tray of them. "So three days isn't anything to panic about. You can't give a bird a datebook."

I thought *You Can't Give a Bird a Datebook* would be a good name for a really boring romantic comedy. I liked Lucille—she was about as normal as a birdhead could be, and talking to her helped alleviate some of my own anxieties about where Annabella was. I remembered the year she was a week late; Mary and I had been thirteen and the entire island had dissolved into near-hysteria levels of panic. I had never thought *that* much about Annabella before, and so I surprised even myself when her lateness affected me to such a degree: I had insomnia, nightmares when I *did* manage to sleep, and I felt anxious all the time.

My mother had crept into my bedroom in the middle of the fifth or sixth night of waiting and sat down on my bed with her jasmine-and-lavender sleeping draft.

"I could practically hear you tossing and turning from the first floor," she'd said, sitting on the edge of my bed and handing me the mug.

"Why do I care so much that Annabella is late?" I'd asked, pulling myself up to a sitting position and sipping the drink.

"She's a part of our history, whether we like it or not," my mother had said. "The Fernweh women are all related. What happens to one of us happens to all of us."

"You don't mean . . ." We had never directly acknowledged it, that this bird might *actually* be my great-great-great-namesake's sister. It was hinted at heavily, sure, but never confirmed nor denied.

"My second cousin could turn into a black cat," my mother had said, as if that answered everything. She'd bent over to kiss my forehead and then slipped the mug out of my hands; I was already falling asleep, so strong was her magic.

"Anyway," Lucille was saying now, "I don't love that she's late either, but I'm not quite ready to panic. We'll all be laughing about this at the festival, just you wait."

Held three weeks exactly from the solstice, the festival started at six in the evening and ran well into the night. In theory it was a celebration of our island's founding, but in actuality, it was called the Fowl Fair, and I think we can agree on what we were really celebrating.

Yes, Annabella had her own festival.

"I look forward to it every year," Lucille continued, taking a bite of her muffin. "I just hope the little darling shows up in time."

"You should play a little hard to get. Maybe that'll piss her off and she'll come looking for *you*," Mary said—I hadn't noticed her come into the dining room. She stood in the doorway, looking pissed off herself, but I doubted that it had anything to do with the birdheads' concerns.

"Ha! You're funny, Mary," Lucille said, and she took her muffin and wandered off. She had a habit of doing that, wandering in and out of rooms and conversations like she'd never quite grasped the concept of saying *hello* and *good-bye.*

"What's your problem?" I asked when Mary had joined me at the table.

"It's been three days, and I haven't made out with Harrison Birdface yet," she said, scowling.

"I believe his last name is Lowry. And also, he's a birdhead. He doesn't care about kissing girls; he cares about Annabella."

"He could care about both."

"There's no precedent."

"There's no precedent because there's never been an attractive birdhead before," Mary argued. She had a point. "What about his sister? Any luck there?"

Actually, Prue had been about as absent as Annabella. I hadn't seen so much as the back of her head since the inn's opening night party.

I shrugged. Mary sighed loudly.

"We're both losers," she said.

"I don't think not having makeout partners makes us losers," I said.

"First of all, it does. Second of all, I have plenty of makeout partners."

"What's it like being so popular? Like just the most popular little flower in the whole world?"

"It's really nice," she said seriously.

And then, like Lucille, she wandered away.

Having exhausted all hope of further conversation, I decided to ride my bike to the town square and visit Vira at Ice Cream Parlor.

The town square of By-the-Sea was actually more like a rectangle, and it was the only place on the island where, looking east, west, north, or south, you couldn't see any water. There was a gazebo and a small playground on the northern end and a farmers' market at the southern end on Sundays. All around the green were the shops and eateries and businesses of the island: the post office, Used Books, Joel's Diner, Ice Cream Parlor, the coffee shop (named Coffee Shop, because apparently we're really boring), etc. The high school and lower-grade schools were at the northern tip of the square, and the town hall was at the southern tip. It was a five-minute bike ride to reach Ice Cream Parlor, the ice cream and candy parlor owned by Vira's mom, Julia Montgomery.

It was Vira's dream, once her mother retired, to take over the business and rename it Skull & Cone. Already she experimented with making her own flavors, slipping them next to the normal stock so customers had a choice between Dutch Chocolate, Vanilla, Strawberry, Pistachio, and Broken Hearts of Lovers (one of her recent creations, which was basically just raspberry and cream and an unexpected dash of cardamom).

I arrived at Ice Cream Parlor at eleven, right when they were opening. Vira wore her unreasonably cute candy-striper outfit (plus white apron and matching hat!) and was busy setting out the ice cream labels next to their corresponding buckets of ice cream.

"Hi, Vi," I said.

"Oh, I'm sorry, are we still friends? Are we talking now? Do we know each other? Did we have a class together once or something?" Vira said. "First you ditch book club and then you haven't come to see me in three whole days."

"Vira, you know how busy the first days of the season are," I said. "I thought of you every minute."

She shrugged, too elbow-deep in ice cream to argue much. "What do you want while I'm in here?"

"Could I have a Bloody Sundae please?"

That was another Vira original, consisting of whatever her flavor of the day was (today: Lies of Our Elders) with plenty of strawberry syrup and whipped cream on top. She made two and joined me at one of the parlor's little tables.

I could tell even before Vira opened her mouth what she was about to ask me, so I beat her to it. "I haven't seen her since the party. Also good to keep in mind: we don't even know if she likes girls."

Vira took a thoughtful bite of her gray-and-white-swirled ice cream. "Well, let me just say that Colin Osmond was *also* sitting on a bench overlooking the very romantic ocean and moonlight thing that was going on, and she chose to sit with you and not him. And everybody says Colin is the cutest boy on the island. I guess. Right?"

Vira didn't pay much attention to gossip like that, especially when it came to romantic stuff (she was, as she'd once put it, "as aroace as they come"), so it was kind of charming that Colin was still on her radar, at least as far as his island sex symbol status was concerned.

I thought about this for a moment. Given the choice between Colin and me, Prue had picked me. "And he was really sitting alone on a bench?"

"Alone, yes."

"And she picked my bench instead?"

"She made a beeline right toward you. We can't be sure yet whether or not she wants to kiss your face, but your chances are looking up."

"I knew there was a reason I liked you," I said.

"My sage, sage wisdom. And also my ice cream," Vira said.

"And also your ice cream, yes."

I took a circuitous route back to the inn, because it was a beautiful day and the sooner I got back, the sooner my mother would find something for me to do. Mary and I didn't have shifts so much as we had two months of being at our mother's beck and call. But it was worth it, as she often reminded us, because in return we got food and shelter and the occasional magic potion.

I ran into a small herd of birdheads just south of the town square, milling about in the parking lot of the town hall

(Annabella had once nested on top of a streetlamp there).

"Anything yet?"

Tank Smith, busy setting up a complicated-looking tripod and camera, looked over and scowled. "Nothing at all. Not so much as a feather."

"Oh, she's here all right," Henrietta Lee chimed in, adjusting her thick glasses on her face. She had a set of binoculars hanging around her neck that were bigger than my head. "I can feel her. Can't you feel her, Liesel?"

Liesel held a series of instruments I couldn't even begin to guess the use of. They were small, metallic, and had a trio of glass balls attached to them, each filled with a different color liquid. She harrumphed at being addressed, but didn't offer anything in the way of an opinion. By Liesl's feet, her birdcat, Horace, regarded me with a look of distrust. I gave him a little wave.

"Well, let me know if you find anything," I said.

"You will be the first to know, Georgina," Tank said. He raised his enormous camera and snapped a photo of me before I could protest. Then, looking at the little screen, which no doubt showed my unready camera face, he added, "Ah. Strange to imagine where all the years have gone. I remember when you were just a babe."

The birdheads—especially the older ones like Tank and Henrietta—were prone to random bouts of reminiscing; I took that as my cue to leave. I waved to Tank and the rest of them and went on my way.

Without really meaning to, I ended up at the graveyard. The one graveyard on By-the-Sea was small and old and quiet—a few of my favorite things. I got off my bike, left it leaning against a tree, and walked deeper into the crooked rows of graves.

In the graveyard, it always seemed to be late autumn.

The perfect season for graveyards.

The dead trees had spilled their dry leaves all over the grass, and they'd billowed against the tombstones in big piles.

I found her sitting on a bench outside one of the mausoleums. Prue. Of course. She held a red cardboard box of fries from Joel's Diner.

In the few days since I'd seen her, I'd kind of forgotten how pretty she was, and now it hit me all over again. She wore a dark-green sundress, and her hair was tied with a silk scarf. She had red sunglasses on, even though it wasn't that bright out.

I walked up the steps to the mausoleum, clearing my throat to announce my presence, because I didn't know a *ton* about flirting, but I knew terrifying someone in the middle of a graveyard probably wasn't the best approach.

She looked up and maybe smiled a little, maybe happy to see me? Or else just really happy with the fries, which was possible, because Joel made some really good fries.

"Hi," I said.

"Hi, Georgina," she replied. She patted her hand on the

bench beside her. I guess benches were now my favorite pieces of furniture, taking the place of beds and rocking chairs. I sat.

"I haven't seen you around much. There aren't many places to hide on By-the-Sea; you're talented," I said.

Oh wait.

Was that creepy or cute? I couldn't immediately tell.

Prue laughed a little and put the fries on the bench between us. "I've been spending a lot of time in the library," she said.

"The library? In summer? Why?"

"I like books," Prue said. "And we had to pack light, so I couldn't bring any. And the library dude is really strict; he won't let me check anything out because I'm 'not a By-the-Seathian, and therefore ineligible to acquire a library card.'" She paused, considered. "Do you guys really call yourselves that? By-the-Seathians?"

"Oh, absolutely not. Stevie is the only one. And he's a stickler for those book rules." Stevie Carmichael, the librarian, acted like he wasn't guarding books, but lives.

"Good. I mean, it's actually a little cute. This whole island is a little cute, you know?" she said.

"How do you mean?"

"Like . . . the one inn, the one diner, the one ice cream parlor, the whole town-green situation. An actual gazebo. A beach called the Beach. A mysterious ladybird whose absence so far has made my brother very anxious."

"When you put it that way . . ."

"It's like a different world here. A very quaint, sort of creepy world."

"Creepy?"

"No offense," she said quickly. "I'll shut up now."

"No, please, don't shut up." Never shut up, never leave my sight, let's move into the graveyard together, some of the mausoleums could actually be pretty homey with the right amount of sprucing. It was just so easy to talk to Prue, like she was a complete open book. And she was funny, and interesting, and her smile was like a small revelation. Like she had invented smiling.

"I didn't mean creepy in a bad way," Prue insisted. "I just meant . . . it's like a storybook. Sort of dark, sort of cute, a little too perfect. Take this graveyard, for instance."

"What about it?" I asked.

"Well, I mean . . . it's *fall*," Prue said. "It is literally fall in this graveyard. Brisk air and fallen leaves, and that *smell*. Does that make any sense?"

"I'm sure it's just a geographical anomaly," I said. "You know, how like some cities are always gray and rainy? I'm sure it's just in some weird position on the island. And so it makes it seem . . ." I paused. I didn't know if eternally autumn graveyards were strange or normal or not. "I've never been anywhere else," I admitted, in way of an answer: I don't know any better.

"Really? You've never been off the island?"

"Nope," I said. "I mean—I'll be leaving in two months, for college. So that will be my first time."

"Wow," Prue said, taking a bite of fry and chewing it thoughtfully.

"I know. It's weird, right?"

"I don't want to say it's *weird*," Prue said carefully. She looked at me out of the corner of her eye and laughed nervously. "All right, it's a little weird, yes. But I've done weird things too! I traveled across the ocean to help my brother chase after a bird. So we've both done weird things."

I thought of the weird things I'd done over the course of my life.

When I was eight I'd had to untangle my sister's hair from the branches of the tree she'd floated into.

When I was ten I'd helped my mother mix a tincture that would make the roses that vined up the side of the inn bloom overnight.

When I was twelve, the year my grandmother died, I sat by her deathbed as she spun hay into gold and told me to put it toward my college fund.

When I was seventeen, I met a girl who'd traveled the world and had the kind of hair you wanted to just touch, just see what it felt like, and who when she talked to you stared so intently into your face that you felt just the tiniest bit like you were going to catch on fire.

"Oh, I don't know," I said. "I've had a pretty normal life until now."

Prue ate the last fry and moved the empty container to her other side. I could smell her hair; it mixed with the salt and the magic on the air and made something new, something unique.

"I don't think anything about your life is normal," Prue said quietly, a little distractedly, like her mind was on something else entirely. After a minute she looked at me and asked, "Do you want to do something tonight? I've been hanging out with Harrison a little too much. I love my brother, but he's currently only able to talk about one thing."

"One bird thing?" I asked, trying to ignore the irritating hammer of my heart and the imminent spike of my expectations, trying to remind myself that more likely than not, Prue was straight and just wanted to be friends.

"One bird thing," she confirmed. "I'll find you around the inn later? If you're free?"

"Sure," I said quickly. "Sure, I'm free."

"Great."

She smiled, picked up her trash, and left me alone in the graveyard to dissolve into a puddle of actual sunshine.

With Verity gone, I was one of only four out lesbians on our very small island. Two of them—Bridgett and Alana Lannigan—were in their sixties and had been happily married for thirty-five years. Wisteria Jones was a year younger than I, and while a perfectly nice girl, there had never been a spark between us. Same with Sally Vane, a bisexual girl in Wisteria's class, and Polly Horvath, who was two years younger and had dated both Sally Vane and Sally's second cousin, Marcus.

But here was the problem with all of that—because I knew everyone on the island so intimately, had grown up with all of them, Prue was basically the first girl I had met who was a mystery. Did she like boys? Girls? Both? Neither? I could only guess, which was proving to be hugely irritating.

Was this what it was going to be like off the island? In two months, when I left for college, was my entire dating life going to be a constant cycle of guessing and getting let down? And although I felt accepted here, I couldn't help but wonder about life elsewhere. Would the people at my college be as accepting as the people on By-the-Sea? Would I know how to do this better? To navigate the weird is-this-a-date-or-isn't-it?

Because even now, even as I reminded myself over and over again that what was happening tonight was probably not a date, I could *feel* the sloppy smile plastered across my face, the highest of hopes building in my chest.

Mary noticed it the second I walked into her bedroom (she was reading comics in her underwear in the middle of the day, hiding from our mother). She made a long, drawn-out noise in the back of her throat that sounded a little bit like she was choking.

"Gross, you have a date with her, don't you? It's not fair that you have a date and I don't. I'm prettier."

She probably was prettier, although as far as womb-sharers go, we really couldn't look less alike.

"It's not a date. Have you tried being forward?" I asked, though even as I said it I remembered who my sister was and, duh, of course she'd tried being forward.

"I all but took my clothes off in the dining room and climbed up on his table to perform a jig," Mary said. Then, raising a hand to her chin: "Do you think that would work?"

"I think that would accomplish many things, yes, including Mom banishing you from the island and burning your name off our family tree."

"But at least I'd have a date," Mary said, like she wasn't ruling it out.

"I don't even know why you like him so much. Is it just because he's fresh blood?"

Mary wrinkled her nose. "That's a decidedly gross way to put it, Georgie."

"But you're not saying no . . ."

"I'm not saying no," she agreed. "There are only so many people on this island, as you are well aware. It's nice to have a couple new faces around here."

"So . . . just go up to him and ask him if he wants to get a coffee or an ice cream or take a stroll on the beach or something. What's the worst that can happen?" I sat on the edge of Mary's bed and started flicking absently through a comic.

"Every time I see him he has his nose buried in a book about birds. These fucking people, I tell you. Up to their eyeballs in feathers. What do they *do* for the rest of the year? Sit around and pine for Annabella?"

"Absolutely they do, no doubt in my mind. You just have to shift his priorities a tiny bit."

"Oh, what, now that you have a date you think you're the dating expert? Are you going to open up a match-maker's business on the island? You're so weird."

"Look—Annabella isn't even here yet; he can't spend *all* of his time out looking for her."

"He can," Mary said mournfully. "Trust me, he can."

"Well, then, maybe you need to shift *your* priorities."

"Meaning?"

"Meaning maybe it's time for you to get a little more interested in Annabella."

"Ah," Mary said, doing the chin-stroking thing again. "Intriguing idea."

"You know practically everything about her: where she likes to nest, what her favorite color is—"

"It's lilac, duh, that's why Liesel only wears purple."

"See how much you have to offer Harrison? Now you just have to show him that."

I could tell she was thinking about it.

"Are you *actually* a dating expert?" she asked after a few

seconds. "Oh, maybe that's your thing, Georgie! Maybe your"—she looked around and lowered her voice for dramatic effect—"*magical power* is being a dating expert!"

"Being a dating expert is not my thing," I said, rolling my eyes.

"Maybe rolling your eyes is your thing."

"I thought we agreed that we weren't going to talk about this anymore."

"If you don't get yours, I'm going to renounce mine. I've already decided," Mary said, suddenly serious, ditching her comic and pulling herself up to a sitting position.

"Don't be silly."

"I've already looked up the spell; it's in Mom's book. It's not hard, I can do it."

"Mom would kill you. And that's not even what I want."

"It's not fair. I can't do that to you. Mine is useless anyway; I've never even gotten more than ten feet off the ground."

"It will grow over time, and you're *not* renouncing it. Absolutely not."

"The night of our birthday. If you don't have yours by then, that's it for me. No more. Renounced. A return to normalcy. You can't stop me."

"You can't *return* to normalcy if you've never *been* normal."

When Mary was finally born, five hours after I was, the doctor had a hard time holding on to her. She kept floating out of his grasp, slippery and wet. Luckily the doctor was already eighty-four at that point and chalked the whole thing up to his budding case of dementia. My mom, overjoyed at Mary's immediate displays of power, became increasingly underjoyed when she realized I was just sitting there like a lump of baby fat. But whatever, she eventually decided that one floating baby was enough. She was already dragging stepladders around the house to pry Mary off ceiling fans and light fixtures; it was nice that I generally stayed where she plopped me.

"You can't renounce yours," I said firmly. "And there are still two months left. Anything can happen."

Mary shrugged. She didn't like being told what to do, and I didn't like the determination I saw in her eyes. It was a little scary.

I didn't have time to dwell on it, though—we both heard our mother's footsteps on the attic stairs at the same time. Our attempt to dive under the bed didn't work; there wasn't room for both of us.

"Mary, put some pants on. Georgina, stop encouraging her. I need you both downstairs," Mom snapped.

"Figure out how to turn invisible," Mary said as soon as Mom had gone. "That would actually be something useful."

Prue found me around eight, as I was dusting and winding countless grandfather clocks in the foyer of the inn.

"Cute apron," she said before I saw her, and I whirled

around so quickly I lost my balance and fell sideways into a Howard Miller. It chimed loudly in defiance, and I picked myself up again, red-faced and unbelievably happy.

"Prue!"

"Fancy meeting you here," she said.

"Is it nice outside?" I asked.

She had a pair of tiny binoculars looped around her neck, and she wore a wide, stiff sunhat.

"It's beautiful out," she said. "I thought we could go down by the water?"

Eighteen years minus two months of living on an island and I had never wanted more to go and look at the waves.

"That sounds perfect," I said. I ditched the feather duster and the apron behind the concierge desk, and we walked out into the evening, which yes, was beautiful: warm and quiet and filled with the scent of the roses I usually hated, but right now adored beyond measure.

I led the way, not to the Beach but to Grey's Beach, which was just north of the inn, where the cliffs dwindled off. Long ago someone had carved steps into the rock face leading down to the sand; it felt a little like descending into a fairy tale. Where tourists avoided the Beach because of the shark attack warnings, they simply didn't know how to get to Grey's, so it was usually equally deserted.

The steps were long and winding and a little claustro-phobic. I glanced back at Prue, and she flashed me a smile so wide I swear the moon got a little brighter.

"Are you all right?" I asked.

"Never better," she said.

I felt rusty and out of practice. Verity Osmond and I had dated for almost five months, but that was a year ago. She'd been the only girl I'd ever dated. I suddenly wished I had paid better attention, taken notes, done *something* to prepare myself for whatever this night was.

Prue and I reached the bottom of the staircase and emerged abruptly onto Grey's Beach, moonlit and loud with waves crashing against the cliffs. She took a deep breath and said, "I think I could get used to living by the water."

We were on the east side of the island; there was no land to see off the coast here, just an endless expanse of ocean.

"It's nice," I agreed, but it would have been more accurate to say, *I don't know anything else.*

When I thought of other places, other cities, they were shadowy and blurred. There were two places you could be in this world: on By-the-Sea or off of it. Like every almost-eighteen-year-old who'd grown up here, I was leaving to go to college. Would I be among those who promptly returned from my rumspringa, or would I be among the far lesser number who created a new life, learned how to live outside of this tiny place?

Prue sat down in the sand, her dress pooling around her, and I lowered myself beside her. "Do you regret traveling so much?" I asked. "I mean—do you wish you had somewhere you could say was *home*?"

"I've always had my brother," Prue said thoughtfully. "I think a person can be a home, sometimes, just as much as a place or a house can. Even though he's a few years older than I am, we've always been close. He looks out for me, you know?" She paused, picked up a handful of sand, let it sift between her fingers. "Do you feel that way about your sister?"

"Yes," I said automatically. I felt that way about her even though she was a bit of a vapid, self-absorbed princess. I felt that way about her even though she could fly (okay, hover) and I could not. I felt that way about her even though she put herself first in every situation and I was so often left behind to pick up the pieces of whatever terrible decision she'd made.

It was the way of the Fernweh women; Mary was certainly not the first Fernweh to be born a little bit nasty. My mother had been an only child, but her mother had been one of three sisters. My grandma Berry hadn't gotten her powers until the day before her eighteenth birthday, and my mother told me that her sisters, Samantha and Matilda, brutalized her for it.

"Why would they be so mean?" I'd almost asked, but then I'd remembered Mary, and how you never really knew what you were going to get: the nice, thoughtful, kind Mary, or the raging evil bitch.

"She's trying very hard to sleep with my brother," she said.

"To be fair, she tries very hard to sleep with a lot of people."

"Good for her," Prue said. "She should do what she wants."

"She does *exactly* what she wants."

"And you? What do you want?"

What did I want? So many things, an impossible number of things. I wanted this beach and this moment to last forever, to never fade away into memory. I wanted to peek inside Prue's brain to find out the answers to questions I didn't know how to put into words. I wanted to kiss a pretty girl on a beach and not have to worry about whether eighteen would come and go and I'd be the first Fernweh woman since my great-great-great-great-great-great-namesake to remain as normal as I currently was. I wanted a hundred million things, but I knew how to ask for zero of them.

I pointed east, across the water, my arm indicting the entire world, the entire known planet.

"What more could I want?" I said.

But I think we both knew the answer to that question was:

Lots lots lots lots lots.

WEEKS LATE

A week passed, and then another, and Annabella still didn't show up. The entire island descended into an acute kind of panic. The birdheads organized groups to diligently comb every inch of By-the-Sea, searching well outside Annabella's usual nesting areas, tearing frantically through places she had never once been spotted in. They went door-to-door asking to check people's attics, people's cellars, people's spare bedrooms and linen closets. I saw little of Prue, as Harrison had employed her as his personal bird-hunting assistant, and the two of them were gone from early morning until late at night, when I sometimes spotted them in the dining hall, raiding whatever leftovers they could find. I was too embarrassed to approach her; part of me worried that she was spending so much time with her brother because she didn't want to spend that time with me.

"That's just silly," Mary said when I told her, late one afternoon as we sat on the porch drinking lemonade mules (Aggie's answer to virgin Moscow mules and what to do with my mother's out-of-control ginger plants). The last non-birdhead guests had departed that morning; we had a party of two due to check in soon.

"You don't know. I don't know. Maybe she didn't have a good time. Maybe she figured out I'm gay and she's staying as far away as she can." I shivered; the weather had turned colder recently and that morning had dawned rather gray and misty and had only gotten more miserable as the day wore on.

"She clearly digs you. Obviously her brother is a serial killer psychopathic meanie face who won't let her have any fun."

Harrison still hadn't shown the least bit of interest in making out with her, despite her best attempts. (Her best attempts: stealing a pair of binoculars from Liesel and prancing around the inn wondering loudly if anyone wanted to go Annabella hunting with her. Harrison had been the only one in the dining room at the time. He hadn't looked up from his cup of tea.)

"She probably doesn't want to lead me on. Ugh, it sucks even more that she's a decent person," I said.

"Look, Georgina, if Annabella had actually shown up when she was supposed to, we wouldn't even be having this conversation, because you wouldn't be able to talk, because you would currently have another mouth on top of your mouth."

"When you put it that way it sounds really gross."

"Kissing *is* gross," Mary said. "Think of all the germs."

Two things I didn't really want to think about: mouth germs and the fact that Annabella still wasn't here. The island felt incomplete without her. My mind thought of all the terrible things that could have happened to her on her journey. Maybe she had hit her head and damaged the part of her brain that contained the instinctual knowledge of migration? Maybe she was flying around aimlessly, looking for land, eventually succumbing to exhaustion and drowning in the waters below?

"Are you fucking thinking about Annabella again?" Mary asked.

"You're telling me that you're not the *least* bit concerned about where she is?"

"She's a *bird*, Georgie. I am not concerned about where a bird is, no. She'll show up or she won't."

"She's not just a bird, Mary, Jesus, even you can't be that cruel."

"You don't really believe that, do you?"

"Of course I believe it. It's the only rational explanation."

"Rational? That one of our weird old relatives turned into a *bird*? Honestly, sometimes I think hanging out with a birdhead's sister has rubbed off on you in terrifying, unprecedented ways. You're one step away from changing your major to birdologist."

"Ornithologist," I corrected her.

"Eww, see?" she said. She had finished her drink; she took mine and sipped deeply.

"She's probably dead. She's never been this late. You wouldn't care if she were dead?" I asked.

"Don't be an asshole, Georgina, of course I'd care if she was dead."

"Every year. Since we were *born*, Mary. Every single year."

"Fuck. Is it raining? That's just great. Everything is great."

Mary went inside, leaving me alone on the porch with two empty glasses. The rational part of me knew that I didn't need to be so bothered about Annabella's absence; she was bound to show up sooner or later, she always did. And the birdheads would calm down, and Prue would have more time to spend with me, and Harrison would relax a little bit, and Mary would finally talk him into making out with her, and maybe everything would go back to normal.

But it was hard to let that rational part of me get too much airtime. Everything felt on edge now, buzzing and sharp to the touch. It couldn't even stay hot on this weird island for more than a week; the weather was as inconsistent as my own moods. Ups and downs, sun and rain.

I stayed on the porch until the new guests arrived, a

young married couple on what they charmingly referred to as a "babymoon." She looked almost ready to give birth, and I was tempted to tell her that babies born on By-the-Sea tended to always smell like salt, always crave the ocean on their skin, always look for the full moon or North Star to guide them home. But instead I said nothing, led them into the lobby, got them their room key, and brought them upstairs while they trailed behind me, arms interlocked, kissing and whispering things to each other that were just past the range of my hearing. I knew already that we would not see them for the entirety of their stay, that they would come down for breakfast, maybe, and sneak enough food back up to their room to last them until evening. I was happy for them, a brief moment of happiness that only increased as soon as I shut their door and turned around to find Prue, like a beautiful deer in headlights, standing outside her room, staring at me.

"Hey," she said, smiling. She looked tired. "New guests?"

"They're on a babymoon."

"Really? That's sort of cute."

"I know." I pointed to Prue's binoculars. "Any sign of her?"

"Nope, nothing." She yawned loudly, covering her mouth with both hands. "Gosh, sorry; I think I've slept for about five hours this week. My brother has based his entire scholarly career on this trip. If he doesn't see Annabella, he's going to have a heart attack."

"She'll show up," I said, trying to sound convincing. "She always does."

"I hope so," she said. "Hey—what are you doing now? Maybe we could take a walk."

The six most beautiful words that had ever been uttered in the English language. Maybe! We could! Take a walk!!!

"I could do that, sure," I said, trying desperately to find some appropriate balance between *unmatched excitement* and *casual, cool indifference.*

"That's great. Let me change quickly? I'll meet you out front."

"Yeah, sure, of course," I said. She slipped into her room, and I tried not to actually skip for joy as I walked back through the inn and took up a post on the porch.

She joined me a few minutes later, wearing a dress with a full sailor's collar complete with a little bow just below the hollow of her neck. It would have looked absurd on anyone else, but on Prue it looked off-handed and sweet. She had one of those old cameras with her, a clunky box that you had to look down into to focus.

"Has it stopped raining?" she asked, holding her hand flat to the sky. "That's nice."

That's because you brought the sun with you to By-the-Sea; it follows you like a doting celestial body, I wanted to say, but miracle of miracles, I managed to keep my mouth firmly shut, choosing instead to only nod and smile, the far, far, far wiser choice.

"Where should we go?" Prue asked.

"I know someplace," I said, and we stepped off the porch together.

The sun was low in the sky, just an inch or two off the horizon. We weren't going far. The big oak tree was a short walk, sitting directly on the southern tip of the island, so close to the edge of the cliffs that some of its roots actually lurched out over the air, and the bravest of souls could climb carefully, carefully out, holding their breath while their friends snapped a picture. I thought it was hilarious, because what I knew that they didn't know was that the cliffs held no danger for them. My mother's grandmother had placed a protection spell on them after a birdhead with his nose in an ornithology magazine had walked straight over the edge to his death. "There are enough ways to die on this Earth," my great-grandmother had famously declared, "let 'distracted reading' be one less thing to worry about."

For the less daredevilishly inclined, there was a tire swing attached to one of the tree's largest branches. At full swinging power, your feet came almost to the edge without going over—if you looked straight ahead and angled your chin toward the sky, it was exactly like you were flying into nothingness, into air, into blue, into clouds. When I was younger I used to think that's what Mary must have felt when her feet left the ground: the soaring, stomach-dropping punch of potential.

When Prue saw the tree, she gasped a little, and then when she saw the tire swing, she gasped again, and she ran the rest of the way to it with her camera bouncing painfully on her hip.

"Georgina! Did you know this was *here*?" She shrieked, and then she laughed and said, "Wait, duh, of course you knew this was here. This is unreal."

The tree was pretty impressive, even to me, and I'd grown up with it. I had seen it and climbed it and hugged it and carved my initials into it and hid behind it. It looked like a tree straight out of a Southern gothic romance; all it was missing was the Spanish moss.

Prue unslung the camera from her shoulder and set it gently on the ground, and then she threaded her legs through the center of the tire swing. I wondered if she would ask me to push her, but she didn't, just backed up slowly on tiptoes and kicked her feet up in front of her, flying forward and back, pumping her legs, gaining speed quickly.

To our right, the sun was just dipping into the ocean. Everything was bathed in orange, peach fuzz, candy apple-y colors that made By-the-Sea seem like something out of a storybook.

"Georgina, come on!" Prue said. She'd dragged her toes into the grass to stop herself, and she was currently waiting impatiently for me to join her. There was not enough room for us both to sit, and so I climbed carefully to the top of the swing, standing straight up on the tire with my hands wrapped around the rope for balance.

And the sun blinked its final glow, and Prue reached a hand up and touched my left ankle briefly, and this, too, must be what flying felt like: stomach-dropping, indeed.

FOWL FAIR

The day of the Fowl Fair dawned to a low buzz of disappointment. There was nothing to celebrate. Annabella still hadn't turned up. She had never been this late before. The island was in disarray, and the inn was the epicenter of its specific breed of chaos. Everywhere you turned there were birdheads in various states of mental unraveling. The energy was cluttered, confused, frantic. It seemed absolutely absurd that the Fowl Fair would continue despite Annabella's absence, but everything had been planned, and we were an island of routine and tradition. It was impossible that we would forgo something as steadfast as the festival.

Willard Jacoby came to the inn to see my mother. He was the mayor of By-the-Sea, the first selectman of By-the-Sea, the town chairman of By-the-Sea, and basically the elected official of everything you could be an elected official of.

I knew what he would ask even before he reached the front door.

He wanted to see if Penelope Fernweh knew how to fix this. If she could throw some things together in a big black pot and magically pull Annabella out of it. "Truth be told," he said, standing nervously on the front porch, "I was hoping maybe your mother . . . well, maybe there's something she could do?"

I had to think that if my mother could have done something to find Annabella, she'd have done it by now, but nevertheless I led Willard into the house and brought him into the kitchen, where my mom was polishing silver (was my mom obsessed with polishing silver? I would have to look into this later). She looked up when we walked in, and I knew she'd figured out what Willard was going to say before he even opened his mouth, just like I had. She made a shooing motion with her hands, an indication that she wanted me to leave, but I hung back toward the door and watched. It was always fascinating to me, seeing the people of By-the-Sea trip over their words in an attempt to ask Penelope Fernweh for a favor. It was almost better than a movie.

"Penny, dear," Willard began. "You know I wouldn't come to you unless it was an emergency."

I actually knew for a fact that Willard had come to my

mother last year when he'd noticed his hair was starting to thin, which could hardly be considered an emergency, and the faintest smirk on my mother's face told me she did too.

"What's on your mind, Willard?" she asked, because she wasn't the sort of woman who just handed things to people. She liked to make them work for it.

"Penny, the people are panicking. Annabella is so late, and . . . well, you know. I thought there might be something you could . . . do."

"You don't think I would have done it already, if there were?"

"I don't know how all this works," Willard said quickly, holding his hands up in front of his chest, like he hadn't meant to offend her. "Maybe I can help?"

"You want to help?" she asked. "Hmm. Well, that's a different story." She replaced the fork she was currently polishing back into its case and wiped her hands free of some invisible dust. She walked over to the coffeepot and poured a mug of coffee. With her back turned, so neither Willard nor I could see what she was doing to it, she fumbled around in a cabinet. She took out small, colored bottles of different things, moved them to the counter, placed them back. When she turned around, she was holding the mug in her hands. Her face had settled into an expression of compassion.

"There's nothing I can do to help find Annabella. She has always been above my abilities," she said sadly. "But there's something you can do. Taste this, and it will reveal the right answer of whether or not the Fowl Fair should continue."

Willard adjusted himself to his fullest height, standing straight and looking important as he took the mug from my mother. He looked into its depths, took a tentative swallow—then a deeper one—and then nodded once.

"Well?" my mother said, holding her hands in front of her like she was eager to hear what he'd learned. "What do we do?"

"The show must go on," Willard announced confidently. He set the mug on the counter. "Penny, I thank you for your help, but there is much work to do!"

He turned and practically ran me over on his way out of the kitchen.

I walked over to the mug, picked it up, sniffed it, and took a cautious taste.

"Cinnamon and vanilla?" I guessed.

"And a bit of myrrh. People love myrrh," Mom said.

"How did you know what he was going to say? What if he canceled the fair?"

"It's Willard. He's not going to pass up the chance for an islandwide shindig. This way, he feels important, I didn't have to cook anything up, everybody's happy. Besides, I see no reason to cancel the fair. I think it might be nice. People need a little distraction. Tensions are high."

Tensions are high qualified for the understatement of the

year; just that morning, Liesel Channing had started crying so hard that her contacts washed right out of her eyes.

My mother sighed loudly and dumped the rest of the unmagical coffee down the drain.

"Are you all right?" I asked her.

"There's a lot on my mind, Georgie," she admitted.

"Like what?"

"Like how long these birdheads are willing to wait before they ask for their money back and get the hell off this birdless island."

"Do you think that might actually happen?"

"I couldn't begin to guess," she said. "It's not easy reading minds. Complicated recipe. Takes too much energy. And besides that, people don't always think the truth."

"But would we be okay? If they did that, would we have enough . . ." It was hard to say the word *money* aloud at the end of a sentence like that.

"Let's just say it was your grandmother who could spin hay into gold, not me. And her gift had its limits too. We have a bit saved up, but not enough to last forever." She paused, put her arm around my shoulders. "Tell me, you haven't been feeling any tingling in your fingertips lately when you see hay?"

"Sorry, Mom," I said.

"I thought not. Ah well. We better pray for a bird-shaped miracle, my love."

❊ ❊ ❊

Mary and I rode our bikes to the town green a little before six. The sight of the town square transformed—food tents, a small area of carnival rides, a little midway with games impossible to win—made me strangely calm. See, we could still function as an island, as a town, sans Annabella. We did not need some magical bird to make us interesting. We were unique all on our own! Look, a festival! An actual, proper, midsummer celebration of life! How very quaint and lovely of us!

Mary and I were on ride duty; our kingdom consisted of a thirty-foot-tall Ferris wheel, a bouncy castle mid-inflation, a little merry-go-round made up of a mermaid, a brightly colored fish, and a blue whale.

"Is this how we die?" Mary mused. "Of boredom?"

"I don't think we're that lucky," I whispered back to her.

Vira showed up soon after with her ice cream cart. She gave us both cups and spoons, and we dug out the flavors we wanted ourselves, praising her good name.

As expected, just about every living soul on By-the-Sea showed up to the festival, anxious and hopeful that something, *anything,* might happen—that Annabella might swoop down from the sky and alight on the gazebo, maybe.

The time passed quickly.

The same few kids rode the rides and bounced in the bouncy castle for hours. Then Jimmy Frankfurter stuffed himself with cotton candy and jumped immediately on the

Ferris wheel and puked at the very top, an impressive spray of sick that landed on the two unfortunate souls in the cars underneath him.

"Holy mother of shit," Mary said when she noticed a few minutes later (having been occupied with a small technical glitch over at the carousel). I was trying to clean up vomit with some paper towels stuck to the end of a broom, because if I got too close to the mess I felt like I was going to puke myself.

"Jimmy Frankfurter," I mumbled. At the last islandwide Halloween party he'd bobbed for and ate so many apples that he puked a brilliant pile of red. I hated that kid.

"Why did you let him on here?"

"I wasn't paying attention," I said.

In truth, I'd been diligently scanning the crowd for Prue; I was ready at the drop of a hat to very casually ditch my post and bump into her.

"Well, I can do the rest of this if you want," Mary offered, which was uncharacteristically generous of her.

"That is uncharacteristically generous of you," I said.

"I could change my mind at *any* moment," she said, and I thrust the broom into her hand without another word.

I wandered over to the bouncy castle and found it filled with more drunk adults than bouncy kids, which is how I knew it must be after nine, the unofficial time when the festival dissolved from a place of good, clean family fun (at least in theory) to one of debauchery.

"If Willard sees you guys, you're gonna get kicked out," I said to the unidentifiable jumble of limbs and feet in the castle. At least they'd taken their shoes off.

I figured now was as good a time as any to turn off the rides for the night (there was something very satisfying about the idea of the bouncy castle deflating around the group of drunk adults now residing within it), and I did so quickly, turning the last few kid stragglers away with the musings of a seventy-year-old woman ("Shouldn't you be in bed? Where are your parents?"). I found Willard by the cotton candy cart and gave him the keys for the Ferris wheel and carousel.

"Another successful turnout!" he said, beaming, clutching the keys in his hands as if they were the keys not only to the kiddie rides, but to *the entire world.*

I decided not to tell him about the vomit.

As the night grew darker, more lanterns were lit, including fairy lights that strung back and forth overhead. This was By-the-Sea in a nutshell: a weird little island with a festival dedicated to a bird who was late to her own party.

When I got back to the rides, the castle was fully deflated, the people within seemed not to have noticed, the vomit was mostly cleaned up, and my sister was gone.

I found Vira with her shoes off, sitting on the grass with her back against the ice cream cart and her legs spread out in front of her.

"We're all out, girl scout," she said, patting the cart.

I sat down beside her. "I don't want your ice cream; I want your company."

Vira put her hand on her chest. "Be still my heart."

"How are you?"

"Tired. Stained with Frozen Blood." An ice cream flavor; she held out her arms to demonstrate.

"Why don't you go home?"

"To be honest, I was just saving up my energy for the trip. I am *tired*."

"I'm tired too. Have you seen my sister?"

"Not for a while," Vira said, shrugging. "I think she was talking to Peter earlier." She put her head on my shoulder and actually started snoring. I resigned myself to being her pillow for at least a few minutes.

And then, there in front of us—not there one moment, there and beautiful the next, was—

"Prue," I said. This single name was meant to convey a lot of things: *Prue, I am so happy to see you* and *Prue, you look so beautiful tonight* and *Prue, if you keep looking at me like that I will have to kiss your entire face, societal etiquette be damned!*

"Hi, Georgina," she said, and I couldn't even begin to translate that into anything more than exactly what it was. A simple greeting? A declaration of love? A hello, a good-bye? The secret of the universe and our purpose here on Earth?

Vira lifted her head and blinked sleepily. "I'm Vira," she said, sticking her hand out. Prue shook it, still smiling, ever smiling.

"Prue. Nice to meet you. That's an interesting name."

"It's short for Elvira. My mom went through a pretty intense vampire phase."

"I was named after a song," Prue said. "Not as fun a story."

"Well, it could have been worse for both of us," Vira said cheerfully. She held her hand up to me, and I pulled her to her feet. She stretched and hugged me. "I better get this thing home." She patted the ice cream cart. "Nice to meet you, Dear Prudence." She winked and was on her way.

"I like her," Prue decided.

"My best friend, of the non-sister variety," I said. "I'm officially done with ride duty—should we go for a walk?"

"That sounds great," Prue said, and we started off across the town green as the Fowl Fair slowly packed up around us. "I wish I could have gotten here earlier, but my brother had me out all day again." She sighed and looked at me. "Still no sign of her. Do you think something bad happened?"

"I don't know. It feels . . ."

Like it.

But I didn't want to say that.

Because saying things out loud imbued them with a

certain kind of power, and I did not want to give power to the idea that something might have happened to Annabella.

"The birdheads are all losing their minds," Prue said. We reached the edge of the green and started walking south. In the moonlight Prue practically glowed. A trick of either the light or my heart, I couldn't be sure.

"She'll show up," I said. I was so used to reassuring people—the birdheads, various islanders who thought I might have some pull in the matter, *myself*—that my words ended up sounding hollow. Even though I wanted to believe them. I *needed* to believe them. What would it mean for the future Fernwehs if Annabella never arrived? What would it mean for the inn, for our livelihood? For the real human woman who had turned into a bird?

"Either way, I'm glad I came here. Bird or no bird," Prue said.

"Oh?"

A translation of the word *oh*:

WHY TELL ME WHY TELL ME WHY TELL ME WHY TELL ME—

"Because I met you," she continued.

"Oh."

A further analysis of the word *oh*:

OHGODOHGODOHGODOHGOD.

"Yeah," Prue said, and she reached over and took my hand and held it, and every star in the night sky blinked brighter and brighter until the world was as lit up and bright as a midday in summer, a blazing wonder of incorrect light levels.

"Is this okay?" she asked.

"Yes!" I said. I shouted? I was talking too loud. I made a conscious effort to lower my voice. "Yes. It's okay."

We kept walking.

We kept walking WHILE HOLDING HANDS.

It felt like a very specific sort of miracle, this hand holding. It felt good and necessary and gentle and real. Neither of us spoke, we just kept walking and holding hands and then we'd reached the inn and we were still holding hands and then we walked around the back of the inn and we were still holding hands, holding hands, holding hands.

We sat on the bench we'd sat on the night of the inn party; the first time we'd really spoken.

And Prue

still

held

my

hand

and the ocean had never looked so beautiful

and the smell of salt had never seemed so warm and good

and I thought:

possibly this is the best night of my life.

"It's really beautiful here," Prue said.

"It is," I said, but what I meant was *you're* so beautiful here.

"If she doesn't show up soon, he's going to want to leave," she said.

"Your brother?"

"He's already searching for the next place to go, the next rare bird he can study," she said in way of an answer.

That stock, empty, fake response again, because I didn't know what else to say. "She'll turn up."

"And if she doesn't?"

She has to.

Prue lifted her feet onto the bench, pivoted, and leaned against me, her back against my chest.

And we sat like that for a long time, long enough for my heart to slow down. And then Prue finally got up and walked closer to the cliffs, the magic cliffs you could not fall off, not even if you wanted to. I got up too, and went and stood a few feet away from her.

And then she said:

"I've been trying to get up the courage to do this for a few weeks now."

And then I said:

"Do what?"

Prue took one step toward me, another step toward me. The grass stretched on for a million miles; it would be years before she reached me. She covered her face in both her hands and took another step. I wanted to move, but I thought if I did that, I would explode. My whole entire body would erupt into stardust. Maybe we aren't meant to be so happy, so warm, so absolutely, batshit joyful. Prue was right in front of me, I could smell her clothes, the lavender laundry detergent the inn provided to its guests.

I raised my hands and closed them around her wrists, gently prying her fingers from her face. Her eyelids were squeezed tight. She needed sleep. I could feel the exhaustion coming off her in waves.

And because she had crossed all of that distance, because she had come so close, I thought I could at least be the one to do the rest of the work, and so I kissed her. Lightly. Like how I imagined a bird would kiss another bird.

And she kissed me back. Like how a bird might ask for more.

When we pulled away, I was light-headed from holding my breath and Prue was smiling.

And I think—I *think*—she would have kissed me again, had Harrison Lowry not chosen that moment to come jogging across the back lawn of the inn, binoculars bumping against his chest and a complicated camera in one hand.

"I've been looking for you everywhere!" he said. "Are you coming or not? Hi, Georgina."

"Hi, Harrison."

"Oh no—Harrison, I completely forgot," Prue said, her

smile disappearing. "Georgina, I'm so sorry, I promised Harrison I'd go out with him again after the festival."

"Looking for Annabella," Harrison explained a little impatiently. "I thought all the lights and sounds might attract her. Plus the fried dough. Hep Shackman told me she *loves* fried dough, but he also talks to his binoculars, so I was taking that with a grain of salt."

"I'm sorry," Prue told me. "I promised."

"It's totally fine," I assured her. "Honestly. I should get some sleep, anyway. Long day."

"I'll see you tomorrow?" she asked, as Harrison sort of hopped up and down on the balls of his feet, looking like he was contemplating whether it would be okay to take her hand and pull her away.

"Definitely. See you tomorrow," I said.

I waited until they had walked back up to the house and veered off down the side of Bottle Hill before I went inside. The inn was empty and so was my sister's room, her bed made sloppily and her pajamas thrown in a pile on top. I collapsed in my own bed, feeling the edges of sleep already pulling me down, the gentle yelling like some sort of lullaby.

The gentle yelling?

I opened my eyes to pale sunlight filtering in through the roses vining past my windows.

It was morning already? I must have fallen asleep more quickly than I thought.

And it was quiet now so the yelling must have come from my dreams—

Except, no, there it was again. Someone in the inn was yelling. Multiple someones, a clash of voices that reached all the way up to my attic bedroom.

I got myself out of bed and pulled on jeans and a T-shirt and, rubbing sleep from my eyes, I walked down the short hallway and pushed Mary's door open.

Her bed hadn't been slept in. It was exactly as I'd left it last night.

I felt a thrill of fear as my brain struggled to put the two things together: the many rising voices downstairs and my sister's empty bed. Had something happened to Mary?

I ran down three flights of stairs and found myself in a lobby filled with people—birdheads, Aggie, my mom, and—

Relief flooded through me as my sister appeared out of nowhere, grabbed my hand firmly, and pulled me around the corner and into the library.

"What's going on in there?" I asked, but she just kept pulling me, into the dining room and around the back of the house to the back porch, down the stairs and onto the grass. She was wearing the same outfit she'd worn to the Fowl Fair. There was a small tear in her shirt. She hadn't slept, and her eyes were big and wide. Her hair was escaping her braids and falling down around her face. "Mary, what is it?"

"I was here last night. Got it? I had too much to drink, and I fell asleep like this," she whispered hurriedly.

"What? What are all those people—"

"Georgie, got it? Do you understand?"

"Fine, yes, obviously I'll cover for you, can you just tell me—"

"She's dead," Mary said.

"What—who?" I asked, and all of these faces cycled through my head, all of the girls and women of the island, starting with Vira and Eloise and Shelby and Abigail and Prue and—

"Annabella," Mary said. "They found her, and she's dead."

"No," I said. "That's not true, Mary, she's not even here yet, she's not even here. Why would you say that?"

But she couldn't reply. I saw her words catch in her throat and I saw her swallow them back down and I saw the tears begin to fall down her face.

I pulled her toward me and felt her heart beat against my chest, a broken beat, something shattered and taped back together.

And as we stood there—

Just like on the day of our births—

The skies opened up.

And it began to pour.

II.

I was a child and she was a child,
In this kingdom by the sea.

also from "Annabel Lee"
by Edgar Allan Poe

DAYS AFTER

If Annabella's absence had brought with it a building sense of panic, her death brought with it a terrifying crash, a cacophony of noise that descended over the island and made our ears ring. I dragged Mary home, leading her up the back stairway and into her bedroom.

"You need to lie down," I told her, helping her into the bed, pulling her shoes off her feet, and letting them fall to the floor.

"I was here all night, okay?" she whispered.

"Fine, Mary, fine. Just don't worry about it, okay?"

I pulled the blankets over her and went downstairs again. The crowd of birdheads had dispersed; I intercepted my mother as she pulled on high, black boots in the kitchen.

"Is it true?" I asked her.

"I know as much as you know," she said.

"But Annabella's dead?"

"I know as much as you," she repeated. She looked up at me then, finally finished with her boots, and I saw that she looked sad, and worried, and maybe a little scared. "They said she's dead, yes. I'm going now."

"Who said she's dead?" I asked.

"Frank and Nancy Elmhurst," she replied. "They found her in their barn."

Peter's parents. They lived near the cemetery.

"I'm coming with you," I said.

"Hurry up and get your shoes on."

We were soaked by the time we reached the Elmhursts' farm. The birdheads had beat us to it; some of them held umbrellas, some of them had rain jackets, but most of them just stood in the open and let the water rush over them.

I should have anticipated what a shitshow it would be. Birdheads were dramatic under the most benign of circumstances; now that they had something to actually be upset about, every single one of them had forgotten how to conduct themselves as adults. There was open, messy weeping, long hugs with no end in sight, low keening moans that started and ended as if from everywhere and nowhere at once, and more yelling—Liesel, her purple dress soaked to the bone, was arguing loudly with Henrietta as the latter fought a losing battle of keeping her thick eyeglasses dry. Horace paced nervously by their feet, ducking in between their ankles and over Liesl's purple rainboots.

"What happened?" I asked Tank, who was sitting

outside the barn, under the overhang of the roof. He had his camera in his lap and his hands wrapped around it like it was the heaviest thing he'd ever had to carry.

"Georgina?" he said, looking up at me slowly. "Please don't go in there. It's terrible in there. I couldn't bear it if you saw."

Hep Shackman, who was just a few feet away from Tank, mumbled something then, and I almost went to him before I realized he was just talking softly to his binoculars, holding them in his lap like he'd gotten confused and thought they were Annabella. When he looked up and saw me, he acted like I'd startled him, like for just a moment he was afraid of me. But then he returned his attention to his binoculars.

"Should somebody call the police?" I asked to no one in particular, because wasn't that what you did when someone died? I tried to remember the practicalities involved in death, and that was the only thing I came up with: somebody should call the police.

"Harrison did," Prue said, suddenly beside me, looking even more exhausted than she had last night and soaking wet. I suddenly remembered the bird-lightness of her lips on mine and felt a pang of anger that that memory was being interrupted by something so sad. "It's really terrible," she continued, lowering her voice, taking me by the hand and pulling me away from Tank. "We were one of the first ones here."

"I have to see," I said.

"Are you sure you want to?" Prue protested.

"I have to."

I walked slowly into the barn, letting my eyes adjust to the dimness. There were three overhead lights, large industrial-looking things that gave out just the faintest whisper of a glow, humming with the effort. There was only one person in here, standing directly in the center of the space, eyes trained on the floor.

My mother.

She took one step to the side and held her hand out to me.

It was worse than I could have imagined.

Annabella was lying next to a thick wooden support beam, broken and small in death. Her wings were spread limply open, as if she had died in an eternal flight. There were clumps of straw and feathers and twigs around her, and it took a moment for my brain to understand what it was—her nest. Her nest was lying in pieces all around her, as if someone had taken it in their hands and ripped it apart.

"Mom," I said. "Did somebody . . . ?"

"I don't know," she said. "It certainly looks that way."

"Her nest . . ."

"I know."

"Harrison called for the police."

"I know."

She knelt down on the dirt floor of the barn and held

her hand over the broken body of the bird, as if she could feel something I couldn't. She plucked a thin straw of hay from the dirt and held it, considering.

"It was an accident," I insisted. "It had to have been an accident. Birds fly into windows all the time, right?"

"I think we both know Annabella was no ordinary bird," she replied softly. She let the hay drop to the floor, and then she stood up and took my hand. "Somebody did this to her."

But I didn't want to believe it. The thought that somebody could have hurt Annabella was so sharp and toxic it made my stomach curl.

I felt something brush against my side, and Charlene Brooks stepped around to the other side of Annabella. She was By-the-Sea's sheriff, a woman about my mother's age with dark-brown skin and short curly hair mostly covered by a baseball hat.

"I didn't want to believe it," she said.

By-the-Sea's one deputy, Whitey, had followed her into the barn. He put his hand over his heart. The four of us stood there looking at Annabella.

"What do you make of it?" Whitey finally said. He was talking more to my mom than to Charlene.

"I don't think this was an accident," my mom answered softly.

Charlene nodded. "The ripped nest. That break there, in her wing." She crouched down and pointed to Annabella's left wing, twisted and stretched at an unnatural angle. "She couldn't have done this much damage herself."

We were silent again.

There was no crime to speak of on By-the-Sea. We were all quiet here; we all liked minding our own businesses and doing our jobs. There was no theft, no assault, no abuse. Until that day, the most Charlene and Whitey had had to do was write out parking ticket after parking ticket, which nobody ever bothered to pay and they likewise never bothered to follow up on. The one jail cell was used by Whitey to take his midafternoon naps. They were utterly out of their element now, moving uncertainly around the corpse, taking notes, taking photographs, and they both looked a little sick. The barn was stuffy, and I imagined that Annabella was starting to smell, the sharp tang of decomposition, even though it was too early for that.

Finally it became too much for Whitey—he clicked the lens cap onto his camera, bowed his head to us and to Annabella, and left the barn.

Charlene took a shallow inhale and turned to us, shrugging. "I have no idea what to do."

"Let me think about it," my mom said quietly. "I may be able to come up with something."

"I don't know about all that," Charlene said, "but I'll take all the help I can get."

Don't ask questions. Don't pry too hard. It was the By-the-Sea way.

Charlene left us alone. My mother inclined her head slightly toward me. "Are you okay, Georgina?"

"I don't know. I don't know what I am," I said.

She took my hand again. My mother's hands had always been firm and cool, but there was something different about them now.

Now, they were shaking.

I hope it doesn't seem strange, the bird funeral that took place the next night, the way the entire island met once again in the backyard of the inn to bury Annabella near the cliff. So she would be close to the water, people said, as if the entire island wasn't close enough to the water. But I knew it was really so she'd be close to *us*, to her once-home of the Fernweh Inn, to her living relatives, to the girl who shared her dead sister's name.

I hope we don't seem silly, the people of By-the-Sea and the birdheads (even though I have made fun of them plenty of times, but I'm allowed), everyone arriving with bowed heads and somber expressions.

I hope I have accurately described the island and all its eccentricities. I hope I have accurately detailed what Annabella meant to all of us: our tiny claim to fame, but even more so than that—she had been one of us.

My sister had avoided me since yesterday morning, emerging from her room only to pee and brush her teeth and find something to eat. She ignored me when I knocked on her door and even though our bedrooms didn't have locks, I left her alone. It's not good to disturb a Fernweh when she doesn't want to be disturbed. Like vampires, you should wait until you're invited in.

Now she stood on the outskirts of the little group that had formed in the backyard of the inn. She wore a tattered, oversized black sweatshirt, and she pulled her hands into the sleeves and hugged her arms around herself.

The funeral was not a huge production. It rained the entire time. The grass was spongy and soft. Everyone held umbrellas over themselves but came away wet anyway. Peter dug the small grave for Annabella. My mother had put the bird's body into a wooden cigar box, and she placed it inside the hole with a tiny sprig of rosemary on top. Then Peter covered the box up with dirt and people just wandered away, unsure of what to do or where to go, unsure of how much grief was allowed when the person you were grieving wasn't a person at all, at least not anymore, but just a little flicker of a bird.

Pretty soon there was a small handful of us left, sitting in the grass in the twilight: Vira, Prue, Abigail, Eloise, and me. Shelby hadn't stayed after the ceremony; she hated things like this, big showings of sadness. My sister had disappeared somewhere after the first fistful of dirt was dropped onto the grave.

Abigail smoked a long skinny joint and passed it around

our lopsided circle. Eloise cried silent tears, wiping at her cheeks every few seconds. Vira put her arm around Eloise's shoulders and squeezed.

Prue sat beside me, as close as she could manage. I didn't know the last time she had slept; her head kept nodding forward. Finally I leaned close to her and said, "I think you need to get some sleep."

"I can't sleep," she said. "I don't feel tired at all."

I stood up and helped her to her feet, and we walked together into the house. I found my mother in the kitchen while Prue waited in the dining room.

"Can I have a cup of tea? For Prue?"

"Tea tea or *tea* tea?" my mother asked.

"The latter."

"Poor girl." My mother poured a mug from a kettle already warmed on the stove. She handed it to me and said, "Make sure she drinks it all."

Harrison had joined Prue in the dining room; they were sitting at one of the tables together and looked more like twins in that moment than Mary and I ever had. Equal in sadness, equal in exhaustion.

I set the mug in front of Prue and then pushed it closer to her when she didn't immediately pick it up.

"It's good for you," I said. "It will help you sleep." *It will knock you literally unconscious* was closer to the truth.

She took a tentative sip, and then another, and then

finished the rest of the mug in one giant gulp.

"Oh," she said when she was done.

"Are you okay?"

"I have to lie down. No. I'm fine. Sleeping. Fine. Immediately."

"Do you need help upstairs?" I asked, but she stumbled out of the room without answering.

Harrison watched her go, bemused.

"I don't think she's gotten much sleep lately," I said.

"Nor have I," he admitted. I realized this was the first time I had been alone with Harrison. He looked completely devastated and suddenly a lot younger than I knew he was. He put his face into his hands and sighed heavily, his shoulders rising and falling. Then he looked at me and rubbed his eyes. "What do you think happened to the eggs?" he asked quietly.

"The eggs?" I thought back to the Elmhursts' barn, to Annabella lying in the dirt with pieces of her nest strewn about her. "There weren't any eggs."

"I know. But I also know that Annabella only builds her nest when she's ready to lay. She's never been found before she's laid her eggs. Not once."

"So what are you saying? That somebody took them?"

"Or broke them, I don't know. I don't know what I'm saying. I just think it's weird they weren't there."

"I don't know who could have done this."

"It couldn't have been a birdhead," Harrison said.

"They all love her too much."

"Hey, you're a birdhead too," I pointed out.

Harrison smiled weakly. "Fine—*we* all love her too much."

"But it couldn't have been an islander. We love her just as much."

"What about that really pregnant woman I've seen darting around here?"

"I don't think the babymooners snuck out of the inn in the middle of the night to murder a bird," I said.

The truth was, I had no idea why someone would want to kill Annabella. She was responsible for the fiscal success of our tourist season, a source of pride, our sole claim to fame. I couldn't imagine anyone on By-the-Sea would have wanted her dead.

"We're the only newcomers here," Harrison said thoughtfully, a little quieter. "It would stand to reason . . ."

"I don't think you had anything to do with this."

"I'm only saying, it would be an obvious conclusion. New birdhead comes to the island; Annabella ends up dead."

"Nobody is going to think that."

"Well, *somebody* killed her," Harrison said. Then he looked at me quickly, a little worried. "I think I'm panicking a little. I don't know. Perhaps I'd better get some sleep too. Is there any more of that tea?"

"Go see my mom," I said, pointing toward the kitchen.

"She'll take care of you."

I went out to the backyard. Abigail and Eloise had gone, but Vira was still there, sitting alone, a dark smudge in the middle of the rapidly darkening night.

She held a bright-yellow umbrella, a tiny refuge against the downpour of rain.

I sat down beside her, and she put her arm around my shoulder.

"Fuck, Georgina," she said.

I couldn't answer her. I had begun to cry, and I thought in that moment I would never, ever be able to stop.

It rained throughout the night. When I woke up, it was still raining and the driveway was under a half inch of water. The door to Mary's bedroom was slightly ajar, so I went in. She was asleep on top of the covers, still dressed in that black sweatshirt from yesterday. I woke her up and brought her into the bathroom, then handed her a towel and ran the bath. She didn't protest, just waited patiently while the water filled and I sprinkled bath salts on the surface, something of my mother's invention that smelled of lavender and camphor and made the room hazy and warm.

I shut my eyes as she undressed and got herself into the tub, and when I opened them she was submerged to her neck, her head tipped back and her hair spilling over the edge of the tub, already damp and frizzy from the moisture in the air. I sat on the toilet so I could make sure she didn't fall asleep and drown. She washed herself methodically with a bar of peppermint soap, raising her arms one by one over her head, lifting her feet gingerly out of the water. Her movements were slow and heavy, like she was in pain. The water was milky enough that I couldn't see into it, but once, when she lifted her neck to wash her face, I saw what I thought was the dark edges of a purple bruise blossoming on her back. When I looked again, it was gone. An effect of my mother's bath salts or a trick of the eye, I couldn't be sure.

When she was done, I handed her a towel and she stepped out of the tub and onto the tile floor. She looked smaller, like she'd lost weight and inches overnight. My poor sister, who loved Annabella as much as I had, who had to imagine, as I had imagined, a murderer flinging the bird against a pole, breaking the fragile, hollow bones that held her together, twisting her wings, ruining her flight forever. I knew that great terrors could shrink a woman, and I knew that my sister would never be the same. That maybe none of us would.

I moved from the toilet so she could sit down, and then I towel dried her hair and combed it with my fingers, braiding it into a long plait that I twisted into a bun on the top of her head. She smelled like lavender, like fear.

"I never knew how much I cared about a little bird," she said when I'd finished with her hair.

"It's all going to be okay."

"She's never nested in the Elmhursts' barn before," Mary

said. "I don't even think anyone looked there. She was in the rafters, high up. They found pieces of her nest up there. Do you think she was hiding because of the weather? It's been raining so much lately."

"I don't know. It's possible."

I imagined someone placing a ladder against the loft in the Elmhursts' barn, taking their time climbing up to Annabella. She was trusting; she was used to people getting too close, taking her picture, measuring her eggs with delicate tape measurers. She would let you put a finger on her head and rub. When she'd had enough, she would nip you ever so gently, like a cat who doesn't want to hurt you but just wants you to leave it alone.

"I keep dreaming about it," Mary whispered. She squeezed her eyelids shut and shook her head back and forth.

I put blush on her cheeks, because I didn't know what else to do, because she looked so pale.

"I think you need some more sleep now," I said.

I brought her back into her room and handed her pajamas, waited while she got dressed and then helped her crawl into bed.

"Is it even bedtime?" she asked, her eyes already closing, her hair quickly soaking the pillow.

"It's bedtime. Look, it's dark outside."

Mary looked to the window, where it was, indeed, dark and gray and wet.

"It feels like I'm still there," she said quietly.

"Where?"

But she didn't say anything, so I covered her and tucked her in, then sat on the edge of the bed while she struggled to stay awake. I didn't know what else to do for her, how to help her. She looked lost, too small, a shrunken shadow underneath the blankets.

"You don't think it's weird, to be so upset?" she asked again, eyelids heavier, face relaxing.

"Of course I don't."

"Because everybody is upset about Annabella, right?"

"They are. You just need a little rest. When you wake up, Mom will make you something to drink."

"You'll get yours, Georgie. You'll get yours or I'll renounce mine," she said, and her eyelids shut with an almost audible, minute crash.

I waited a few minutes just to make sure she wasn't going to get up again, and then I pulled all the curtains shut and turned the lights off and closed the door behind me when I left.

I got dressed and went downstairs. The inn was packed with people but eerily silent; the birdheads didn't know what to do with themselves, so they were eating a very long and slow breakfast, and Aggie was quickly running out of food.

I made myself a plate of pancakes and went into the kitchen, where my mother was sipping a cup of coffee and picking at a muffin.

"Is your sister still asleep?" she asked when she saw me.

I nodded and poured myself a cup of coffee. I looked down at the brown liquid as I raised the mug to my lips and paused. "What about if you put something in everyone's drinks? And if they're a murderer, their hair would turn blue?"

My mom smiled and touched my own hair. "It doesn't work quite like that. Any kind of big thing like this . . . It takes a bit of planning. A lot of time, energy."

"But you're working on something?"

"I'm working on something, yes, Georgina."

"And how long do you think it will take?"

"A few weeks, at least."

"Weeks?"

"The moon needs to be good again. These are difficult things to do; they take time."

"And until then?"

"Until then, I don't know. Maybe Charlene will come up with something."

"And the birdheads? What if they leave? What if the *murderer* leaves?"

"If anyone attempts to leave the island, they will find the ferry to be quite nonoperational," she said quietly.

So my mother had broken the ferry and trapped us all on the island with a bird murderer. Probably not the route I would have taken, but I didn't exactly have anything to contribute, at least not in the way of magic. I had no choice but to wait until the moon was good again, to see what else my mother had up her sleeve, to hope it would be enough to figure out who had killed Annabella—and *why*.

That was the most frustrating part; I couldn't begin to imagine what sort of motive they might have. And what if it *was* an islander who had done it? Did that make things better or worse? Worse, undoubtedly, because that meant that someone I'd known my whole life had an evil in them that I had never even noticed. My brain cycled through islanders' faces. I wasn't even hungry anymore; I left the pancakes on the counter and took my coffee out to the front porch. Everything on the porch should have been soaking wet with the downpour, but the cushions were warm and dry. My mother's doing, no doubt. And I had a feeling she'd done something to the coffee, as well, because the warmth it provided spread quickly through my body and left me with a feeling just shy of utter relaxation. I bet she'd slipped in a little valerian root, a sprinkle of chamomile, a few muttered, quiet words; just enough to calm down the birdheads who would otherwise surely be beside themselves right now.

If I'd had any bit of real magic of my own, I'd summon up whoever'd killed Annabella and . . .

But I didn't.

So it was pointless to consider.

I was almost finished with the coffee when Peter showed up. I hadn't seen him since the funeral, and there was something about him now, some straightness to his back, a somber way he walked. Annabella's death was affecting all of us differently, I knew. It was like we were all strangers now.

"Hi, Peter," I said.

"Hi, Georgie," he said.

"She's asleep."

"Good. She needs her rest." He swung a wicker end table over with one hand and sat down.

"Are you doing okay?" I asked.

"I don't know how I'm doing," Peter said honestly. "The whole thing . . ." He shook his head, wrung his hands together. "I just wish I could do something to help."

"We'll find whoever did this," I assured him. "The truth will out."

"Tell her I stopped by? I was supposed to do some work in the gardens today, but . . ." He motioned at the rain. "I just want her to know I'm around. If she needs me."

"Of course." Though I couldn't imagine my sister ever needing Peter.

Peter left, replaced quickly by Henrietta Lee, her thick glasses askew on her face, who moved so soundlessly that I didn't notice her until she had sat herself in the chair next to me.

"Geez, Henrietta!"

"I'm sorry, Georgina. I thought I'd get some air."

Henrietta was a tall, thin woman, a reed of a woman.

She'd celebrated her seventieth birthday last year, and Aggie had made her a cake in the shape of an airplane, for her late husband, who'd been a pilot. She was quiet, gray-haired, aloof. She generally stayed to herself, and I don't think she needed much sleep anymore; I'd caught her in the living room at three in the morning, reading books about ornithological case studies in the near dark. Whenever I tried to turn on a light for her, she'd said there was no need: she knew the books by heart.

"Then why hold them at all?" I'd ask.

"They're a comfort. Plus, it'd be a little weird sitting alone in the dark without a book."

I tried to imagine Henrietta killing Annabella, but the image felt immediately wrong to me. I had seen Henrietta scoop spiders into the palm of her hand and walk them outside to the grass to live another day. I had seen Henrietta cry buckets of silent tears at the end of every summer when Annabella's eggs refused, yet again, to hatch. There was no way on this green earth that Henrietta had anything to do with Annabella's death. It just wasn't possible.

"Strange weather we're having," she said, looking out over Bottle Hill. "It's like the island itself is in mourning. Feels a little . . ." She trailed off and looked at me out of the corner of her eye.

I could fill in the blank.

Feels a little spooky.

Feels a little magicky.

Feels a little unnatural.

"Nobody checked the barn," she said after a pause. "She's never nested there before. She could have been there for days. She could have been there all this time, just nestled up high in the rafters, waiting for her eggs to hatch, with nobody the wiser."

"It's not your fault."

"Oh, I know that. It's not anybody's fault." She paused, laughed—but a sad laugh. The saddest laugh I'd ever heard. "Well. It's someone's fault."

I didn't like the way she said it. But I couldn't quite pinpoint why.

She rose from her seat without another word and walked back into the house. I swear, none of the birdheads knew basic conversational etiquette, like *hello* and, God forbid, *good-bye*.

I took my empty coffee mug back inside. My mother was in the kitchen still, sitting by the window, finishing the pancakes I'd left behind.

"You shouldn't drug people," I said.

"I've hardly drugged anyone," she said without looking up. "You can buy those herbs anywhere. And you seemed fine with it the other night, bringing tea to Prudence and her brother."

"That was different." I stole back a forkful of pancake. "Mom . . . Harrison said something last night, and I thought it was a little weird. But you know how Annabella only builds her nest when she's ready to lay her eggs? Well . . . where *were* they? They looked all over the barn, right?"

"I've been wondering that myself," she said quietly. "Yes, they looked all over the barn. They didn't find anything."

"So what does that mean? Why would somebody want a couple of useless eggs? They never even hatch."

"Why would somebody kill a beautiful thing like Annabella?" she asked. "Why do these people do anything they do?"

When my mother said things like that—*these people*—I think she meant everyone in the world who wasn't a Fernweh.

FLOOD

My mother's coffee had made me sleepy, but not in a tired way, in a sad way, a mournful way. I wanted to lie down, to close my eyes, to try and forget about Annabella for a while, only my room seemed too empty and lonely, so I went to check on Mary. I found her floating at least a foot off her bed, which proved my theory about why her mattress was so much more comfortable than mine (less use) and *also* seemed a bit dangerous to me; surely her freshman roommate wouldn't be as understanding about a floating girl?

But now that I was up here I realized I wasn't tired anyway, I just didn't want to be alone. I tugged on Mary's arm until she woke up and fell back on the bed.

"Is it tomorrow yet?" she said, sitting up.

I unbraided her hair, still damp and now falling curly down her back. "It's the morning," I said.

Mary stretched her arms out and said, "I had a dream I was flying."

"That's not a bad dream to have," I said, still unbraiding. "Peter came by to see you."

She sat up straighter in bed. "Is there coffee made?"

"Yeah, but I'd make your own pot."

"Tainted?"

"Definitely tainted."

Mary swung her legs over the side of the bed but didn't make any immediate move to stand. Instead, she looked at her feet and the floor beneath them, a good six inches away.

"Mary?"

She shook her head, smiled, looked at me, and gingerly put her feet on the ground. I saw an unmistakable wince on her face, the slightest giveaway of discomfort.

"I'm just a little sore," she said. She used my shoulder to lift herself up and then swayed gently, as if caught in a breeze.

She really did look smaller, and like her features had resized themselves appropriately.

"You're still floating," I said.

She looked down at her feet and laughed gently, a laugh not unlike the trill of birdsong.

"What would I do without you?" she said.

"Be burned at the stake."

"Or crushed to death with rocks."

I tried to smile, but really I was thinking about Mary's college roommate again, and about how my sister was no closer to being able to control her powers than she was when she was a kid, getting stuck on the ceiling in the living room or tangled up in the branches of a tree.

Then she winked, and she was Mary again, no longer something more fragile and lost than the sister I'd grown up with. She left me alone in her room, and I sat on the bed, feeling the coolness of the blankets that hadn't been slept in. I lay down, folding my arms behind my head, shutting my eyes, and taking a deep breath of rose-filled air.

The roses were out of control this year. Peter trimmed them, cut them back, but they just kept persisting. They were thriving in this rain; if we weren't careful, they'd take over the entire house. You wouldn't be able to see anything of the Fernweh Inn except bloodred blooms and dark-green vines and sharp little thorns. Like Sleeping Beauty stuck in a tower surrounded by things that could prick. Except there weren't any princes on By-the-Sea. We didn't need princes; we saved ourselves.

"Georgie?" came Vira's soft whisper from the doorway.

I heard her walk over to the bed and felt the mattress dip as she sat down next to me. I scooched so she could lie down, then I opened my eyes and looked at her. Vira's signature cat eyes were smudged, like she'd been rubbing her eyes. Her hair was knotted into a bun on the top of her head. She wore black lace gloves, and she smelled like rain.

It was still coming down; the attic was filled with the patter of water hitting the roof and running down the windows.

"The streets are starting to flood," Vira said, nudging her chin toward the outside, toward the enormous double windows that faced the front yard.

"Really?"

"Just an inch or two. I saved a kitten on my way over here. It's in the kitchen now; Aggie is trying to feed it cucumbers. I think I'll name it Rain."

"Poetic."

"What are you doing in Mary's room?"

"I didn't want to be alone."

"But you *were* alone."

"Now I'm not," I said, and snuggled against her side. "I sent out a siren call to you, and then you appeared."

"The ferry's broken," Vira said.

"That was my mom."

"I sort of guessed." She turned so she was on her side, propping her head up with her hand. "Is she . . ."

"She's doing something; I'm not sure what. She said she had to wait until the moon was good again."

"Mysterious."

I rolled onto my side too, so we were facing each other. "I think something is going on with Mary," I said. "She seems . . . this is going to sound weird."

"I've known your family my entire life; it sort of takes a lot to faze me now."

"When I look at her I just get this feeling, like . . . I don't know. She seems smaller. She wasn't here the night Annabella was . . . the night she died. She told me not to tell anyone. I don't know where she was."

Vira fell onto her back again. She considered what I'd told her with a serious expression on her face, her forehead a mess of wrinkled lines.

"You don't think she . . ."

"Of course not," I said quickly.

We let the sound of the rain drown out the silence that filled the room.

Of course I didn't think that.

I just didn't know what I thought.

According to Fernweh legend, seven days after Mary and I were born, the rain finally stopped. The entire island was covered in water, five- and six-feet deep in parts. Aggie picked us up from the hospital in a small rowboat. My father and the rest of his crew were still missing; they'd searched the waters off the eastern coast of By-the-Sea every day for seven days and come up with not even a scrap of clothing.

Emery Grace put my mother into a wheelchair and wheeled her to the front door of the hospital, where Aggie waited in her little boat, one hand holding on to the wall of the hospital to keep the boat in place. My mother handed her babies to Aggie one at a time, and Aggie tucked my sister and me into a wicker basket stuffed with blankets. She rowed us all home with powerful, deep strokes.

Back then, our nursery was on the first floor, next to my parents' bedroom. Aggie and my mother tucked us in our cribs and then went onto the porch.

"I'm so sorry, Penny," Aggie said.

My mother's face was stoic, unreadable.

I knew all this because Aggie had told me, because my mother had told me, because I'd dreamed it. Fernweh history belongs to every Fernweh woman. I knew what my great-grandmother ate for breakfast fifty years ago on a random Tuesday in March. I felt the tightness in my mother's chest as she stood on the porch of the inn and looked out at an island drowned and soggy and colorless.

"I'll have to build a widow's walk," she said, and then she looked at Aggie and smiled so Aggie knew that she could smile, too, that the rest of their lives wouldn't be all sadness and loss.

And she did build a widow's walk.

And she never once used it.

Until now.

My mother, sick of birdheads clogging up every room of the inn, procured a sizeable collection of umbrellas from who knew where and kept them in a row at the front and back doors. The birdheads made use of them at once; it was unnerving to stand at my bedroom window and look down at them over the lawn of the inn—dozens of little black umbrella spots of mourning. The entire place was quiet, eerie, still.

I went around and opened every single window in the inn, trying to let out the stench of grief.

But grief was stronger than rainwater, so I didn't think it did much good after all.

I found my mother at the very top of the house, at that very widow's walk she'd built almost eighteen years ago and never used.

The stairs were pulled down from the attic ceiling hall-way. That's how I knew where she was. I climbed up to meet her, emerging into the gray, wet morning. She was holding a large umbrella and drinking a cup of coffee. It was steaming hot, and she gave me a sip without asking. It warmed every inch of my skin. I pressed myself against her side and handed the mug back to her.

"I wouldn't have thought I'd feel so sad," she said. "With Annabella gone. But she was one of us, I suppose, even though we only knew her in a peculiar way." She meant as a bird, and not as a woman who had learned how to grow feathers. "I've heard so many stories about her. From my great-grandmother," she continued. "She lived to be one hundred and six, my great-grandmother. I was named after her."

The original Penelope Fernweh, whose portrait hung

in the library with every other Fernweh woman who had lived on the island and on Bottle Hill and in this house. That Penelope Fernweh had been a storyteller, and she'd left behind journals filled with the history of the Fernwehs— thick, heavy tomes that served as a reminder of the past.

"What was she like?" I asked. "Annabella?"

"She was just an ordinary girl," my mother said, as if that meant anything at all. In a family full of girls, you realize quickly that no girls are ordinary. Whether or not they turn into birds, girls could fly and make magic all their own. But I knew what she was trying to say—that Annabella Fernweh, before she was *the* Annabella, *our* Annabella—was just a girl who, like my sister, sometimes floated an inch or two off the ground.

"Tell me about her," I prompted. Unlike Penelope Fernweh the First, my own mother took a little prompting to open up. She sighed now, took a long sip of coffee, and began.

"Well, you know she was a twin. Annabella and Georgina. I had never planned on naming you after any of us, but I just loved that name so much. I thought there was something poetic about naming you Georgina, about being a better mother to you than Clarice was to her girls."

All I knew about Clarice Fernweh, the mother of the twins, was that she was a dark smudge on the history of the Fernweh name. She kept her girls on leashes so short they were rarely allowed to leave Bottle Hill. They were homeschooled, locked in their bedrooms at night, and not allowed to have any friends.

No wonder Annabella turned into a bird.

"When I was pregnant with you, I used to read Penelope's journals over and over again," my mother continued. "There's a story, about the three of them—Clarice was like me, you know, she could make things, except she wasn't very good at it. She got her concoctions wrong all the time, it got to the point where, if you knew better, you wouldn't even accept a cup of coffee from her. One night, she forgot to lock her daughters in their room, and they took their chance and escaped for the night. They were just teenage girls; they wanted to go explore their island and have some fun and see the ocean at night."

She paused. Her eyes burned with anger at this woman who'd lived so long before her. "Clarice was waiting for them when they got back. She had two cups in her hand, filled with some terrible, smoking liquid. It's a very tricky mixture, to get people to tell the truth. Even I have trouble with it. But for someone like Clarice, it was a disaster waiting to happen."

My stomach felt tight; I had never heard this story before. "She made them *drink* it?"

She nodded, her mouth tight. "Every drop."

"And what happened?"

"Annabella's drink had come out all right. She told her mother exactly where they had gone that night, exactly who they had seen. But Georgina . . . something in her drink turned against her. She grew gravely ill. She was only sixteen, and people say it almost killed her. People say . . . that maybe if it hadn't been for that night, she would have found her powers."

My heart felt like it had shrunk to half its size. I couldn't believe I hadn't heard this story before. Clarice had been a *monster*.

"That's terrible," I said.

"Magic is never guaranteed in this world, not even for a Fernweh," she replied. "I think Clarice wanted to protect her children so much that she ended up ruining them. One of them flew away, and the other . . . Well, if you a stifle a child, you stifle every part of them. Who knows what Georgina could have been if she'd been given the chance to shine. Who knows. She could have been as amazing as you are."

She put her hand on my cheek, and even as she smiled at me, a little voice in the back of my head reminded me that I hadn't found my powers either. I was no better than the original Georgina.

Well—at least I didn't have Clarice for a mother. Magic wasn't everything, not even for a Fernweh.

"I'm so happy you're normal," I told her.

She laughed. "I think that's the first time in history a teenager has ever called her mother normal. I'll take it."

"What about this?" I asked, gesturing out at the rain,

my head still reeling from everything she'd told me. "What do you think is causing this?"

She thought for a moment, letting her coffee cool, staring out over Bottle Hill. "The first Penelope could control time. Nothing too severe. She could pause things for a few minutes, maybe speed up a day if she felt like it. But my mother told me that whenever she did it, things got a little wonky on the island. Using magic always has consequences. It rained frogs once. All the roses bloomed in winter. That reminds me a little of this."

"Are you saying all this rain is a consequence of using magic?"

"A consequence, a result . . . I'm not sure yet. But it smells like magic, doesn't it?"

She turned to face the backyard of the inn, which had been transformed into a memorial for Annabella. Her grave was marked with a little flat piece of wood sanded smooth by Peter, and although the islanders of By-the-Sea were not, as a rule, religious, there were still offerings left: old coins and pots full of seawater and small mounds of beach sand.

My mother had tolerated these gifts until they became too cumbersome, until half the backyard was taken up by trinkets and tchotchkes, and then she went out and collected the items in a cardboard box, which she left on the front porch. When people complained, she said, "I don't dance naked in your backyard," which made them a little confused and a little uncomfortable but also a little less likely to leave their old junk at the inn.

Still, it did not escape me: how strange it was to sit by the grave of a bird who had been so much a part of your identity as a Fernweh woman, and as an islander, that her sudden absence felt like a loss so sharp and profound that it took the place of even your father, of even your grandmother, of even every Fernweh woman who'd come before you and every Fernweh woman who might come after.

Except Clarice.

I don't think I could count Clarice in my mental list of ancestors anymore.

"I'll find who did this," I said.

My voice sounded more confident than I felt. My mother handed me her umbrella and kissed me on the side of my head. She left me alone on the widow's walk; I looked down at the backyard and the smattering of people taking turns crying by Annabella's grave.

Peter had carved into the wood of the grave marker: A.W.

Annabella's Woodpecker.

Secretly I thought he probably should have made it A.F.

Annabella Fernweh.

Once a Fernweh, always a Fernweh, no matter how far you flew.

SUSPICIONS

started to notice something unexpected.

It began as a whisper in the inn, a low murmur that followed me through the halls and crept around corners and slunk in between the sheets of my bed, waiting for me. It began with Shelby leaving Annabella's funeral and casting distrusting looks at my sister. Then Hep Shackman, sitting outside the barn, looking scared when he saw me. I would enter a room and it would fall silent. I would sneeze and everyone nearby would jump. I would cough into the crook of my elbow, and if someone was sitting at the table next to me, they would get up and move.

I thought I was being paranoid at first.

But then I saw Lucille sitting alone in the library of the inn, reading a book about the stages of grief, and when I sat next to her and said hi, she smiled politely, placed the book on an end table without marking her place, and left the room.

My sister wandered in shortly after. She took Lucille's place, crossing her legs under her body, looking like a small child in the overstuffed chair.

It was twilight and there were heavy bags underneath her eyes. I realized I hadn't seen her in days; she had been walking around the house from shadow to shadow, like something that didn't want to be caught.

"Why do you look like you just saw a ghost?" she asked. Then, looking around, "There *are* ghosts here, you know. Vira told me once."

"She was just trying to scare you."

"I don't know. I trust Vira when it comes to creepy things."

"Hey, have you noticed . . . ," I said, but stopped, because I couldn't figure out how to phrase what it was I wanted to say.

Have you noticed people are avoiding us?

Have you noticed nobody will talk to us?

"I passed Lucille in the hallway," Mary said. "She practically climbed the wall to get away from me. So yeah. I've noticed."

"What do you think it is?"

"You know what it is, Georgina, you just don't want to admit it to yourself, because it sucks too much," she said.

She pulled two cookies out of the pocket of her dress and handed me one.

"They think we've got magic," I whispered.

"They've always thought that," Mary corrected. "But now they think I've killed Annabella."

This small crumb of knowledge had been sitting low in my stomach, wiggling around in my gut, trying to get my attention. To hear Mary say it out loud made it real. They thought—the birdheads, the islanders—that my sister killed Annabella.

"It's not fair," I said.

"You can ask me," Mary offered. "I won't be offended."

"I never for one second—"

"Right, but it's fine if you did. I can see how it makes sense. I'm a bitch. People love blaming bitches for things. And plus—you don't know where I was that night."

"You're a bitch, Mary, but you're not a murdering bitch."

"*Murdering Bitch* will absolutely be the title of my memoir," Mary said. She popped the last bit of her cookie into her mouth and chewed slowly.

"Well, where *were* you that night?" I asked.

"At the Fowl Fair. With you."

"And afterward?"

"Here and there," she said, and her expression clouded over. "Do you want to go out tonight? Colin Osmond is having a party."

Even under the black stain of death, the island loved its parties.

I shrugged. "If you want to go, I'll go with you."

"I want to go," she said. "Can you believe it's almost our birthday?"

"Why won't you tell me where you were?"

"I didn't kill Annabella."

"Mary, I would never think that."

"I'll meet you in an hour, okay?"

And she got up. And she floated across the room. And I knew I should go and yank her back to the ground, but instead, I just watched her leave.

Mary knocked on my door an hour later, and didn't wait for me to respond before she let herself inside. She was holding an umbrella, and she'd changed into black, ripped jeans and a boxy T-shirt, heavy black boots that I thought she must have stolen from our mother's closet. Her blond hair was braided into two long plaits that lay over each of her shoulders and she wore a dark plum lipstick that matched the circles underneath her eyes.

My sister always wore long, flowy dresses and not a stitch of makeup. I wasn't sure who this was, but she looked more like Vira or my mother, twenty years ago.

"Is that what you're wearing?" I asked.

"Is that what *you're* wearing?" she shot back. I had on jean shorts, a flannel shirt. My hair was pulled into a bun, and I wore plain white sneakers, dirty now from years of use.

It had taken me the full hour to decide what to wear. What if Prue was there? I doubted the news of a party at Colin Osmond's house would have reached her, but if it *had*, I didn't want to look like I'd gotten dressed up for her, but I didn't want to look like a jerk either. Half my wardrobe was spread out across my bed, and I saw Mary sneak a glance at it.

I hadn't told her about Prue and me kissing in the backyard, but in my defense, I hadn't seen more of her lately than the back of her head disappearing around corners. And I would have told her then, but there was something so disconcerting about the way she was dressed, about the plum lipstick that colored her pout into something unrecognizable. Something a little creepy.

"Are you ready?" she asked, crossing to my window and lifting it open.

I thought of Clarice Fernweh barricading her children in their bedrooms. I thought of the original Georgina so sick with accidental poison that she almost died. I thought of Annabella, seizing her one opportunity to get away forever.

I didn't blame her. Given the chance, I think we all would want wings.

"Georgie?" Mary said. She already had one leg out the window, and she was ducking her head to get outside. I

he said, but I didn't get a chance to respond, because Billy Kent erupted from the house in a mess of alcohol fumes and noise. He seemed to pause midstride when he saw me, a burst of laughter dying on his lips as he pulled the front door shut behind him and froze.

"Oh," he said. "Georgina. I didn't realize you would be here."

"Georgina is my friend," Colin said, putting his arm around my shoulders in a protective way that set me immediately on edge. "Why wouldn't she be here?"

Billy rolled his eyes, but then he seemed to catch himself. He took a slow breath. "I don't know. I guess I just thought she might have other things to do."

"Other things to do?" I asked. It took me a minute to catch on, but then I had a flash of Lucille falling all over herself to get away from me, of Shelby leaving the funeral early, and something clicked together. "Are you kidding me?" I hissed. "Billy, you've known me my entire life."

"Have I?" he said. He was drunk; I could tell by the way he swayed almost imperceptibly back and forth, by the way his eyes didn't quite seem to focus. "Because right now it feels like I've never really known you at all."

"Oh, give me a break—" I said, shrugging out from under Colin's arms. "Don't worry, I'm not staying. Let me just get my sister and we'll both go."

"Your sister? Mary isn't here," Colin said.

Billy recoiled further at the mention of my sister, and a

big part of me wanted to whisper some singsongy mumbo jumbo in his general direction and see how quickly he sobered up, afraid I was turning him into a cat or a frog. But then Colin's words caught up to me, and I looked at him.

"What do you mean she isn't here? She was just ahead of me."

Billy opened his mouth to speak, but Colin stepped in front of him, pushing him bodily away from me.

"Enough, dude," Colin said, disgusted. "Yeah, I don't know, Georgina, but I've been out here for a few minutes. She's not here."

"Fine. What about Vira? Is Vira here?" I asked.

Colin shook his head. "She's not either, sorry."

"Great," I said. I reached behind him and plucked my umbrella out of the stack.

"Georgina, wait—"

"It's fine, Colin," I snapped. "Everything is fine. Enjoy your party."

I opened the umbrella and stepped out into the rain, ignoring Billy's jeers and Colin's attempts to both call me back and shut him up. My body felt hot with anger—at Billy Kent and every person who shared his opinion, and at my sister, for inviting me to this party in the first place and then vanishing without a trace.

I didn't even realize where I was going until I was halfway to the town green, to Ice Cream Parlor and the small two-story apartment above, where Vira lived with her mother, Julia.

I didn't meet a single soul the entire way, and the water came up to my shins and soaked my sneakers and splashed up my legs until I was soaked to my waist. I had a single word stuck in my head and it played over and over to the tune of every nursery rhyme my mother had ever sung me.

It was the word they had called all the Fernweh women before me. The word they would call all the Fernweh women after me. The word that could seem like either a blessing or a swear, depending on how you said it.

When I got to Ice Cream Parlor, it was closed. There was a funny sign on the door, handwritten by Vira:

closed due to inclement weather; also, stop being assholes

I felt my heart swell with love for my best friend because I knew that second part was directed at all the people like Billy Kent and Lucille Arden, all the people who were suddenly convinced we must have had something to do with Annabella's death.

I walked around the building to the metal stairs that snaked up the back, leading to the second floor and the door to the Montgomerys' apartment. I knocked a little melody on the glass windowpane and Vira appeared a second later. She scowled when she saw me but she flung the door open, reached a hand out, clamped down on my wrist, and pulled me inside.

"I've called you a thousand times in the last three days. Did anyone see you come up here? Geez, you're soaked."

"Nobody saw," I said. "There isn't anybody out there *to* see."

"Good."

"What do you mean, *good*?"

"Sorry. But I think I'm the only person on the entire fucking island who hasn't lost their mind. Aside from you, probably. Unless you *have* lost your mind since I saw you last. I wouldn't really blame you."

"People are avoiding you because they know you're my friend," I guessed.

Vira rolled her eyes, which was always an impressive sight, because she could get them so far in the back of her head that only white was left. "I'm so sorry, Georgie. On top of everything."

"Your mom?"

"I've been working on her. But it's me against the whole world, you know? Thankfully she's not here right now."

"I think I'm uninvited to book club," I said.

"Eloise is sympathetic to your cause," Vira countered. "Shelby and Abigail can go fuck themselves."

She steered me farther into the apartment, finally pressing my shoulders down until I was sitting in one of the yellow plastic chairs around the kitchen table. The Montgomerys' home was a strange, strange place. The entire decor was 1950s and very bright and cheery, but Julia, a taxidermist in her spare time, had filled the apartment with every animal that had died on By-the-Sea during the last twenty or so years. The centerpiece on the table was a family of squirrels, perpetually frozen in a snugly, sleeping bundle of bones.

Vira got me a towel and then poured me a cup of tea from a teapot that had been warming on the stove. She sat across from me and watched as I half-heartedly toweled off and then tried a sip of the tea.

Vira in this kitchen would never get old to me. Her black dress, her black hair, the tiny silver stud in her nose— all of that set against the backdrop of bright yellows and blues and oranges was at once both alarming and deeply satisfying. The one place I felt more at home than home was sitting with Vira in her kitchen.

The tea was citrusy and light. Vira made her own tea of herbs she grew in a small garden on the metal landing outside her bedroom window. The rains had probably ruined it now.

"First things first," Vira said. "Did she?"

"No."

"You're sure?"

"Yes."

"I don't *like* asking. But I have to ask."

"I know."

Vira sipped her tea thoughtfully.

"I promised my mom I would find out who killed her," I said. "But I don't know where to begin."

"'Begin at the beginning,'" Vira recited, "'and go on till you come to the end: then stop.'"

"*Alice in Wonderland*? I don't know what that means."

"Sure you do. You're here, aren't you?"

"I don't know where I am," I said, brushing away a tear that was making its way down my cheek.

Oh.

I hadn't meant to cry.

"Georgina," Vira said, producing a tissue from a quaint ceramic tissue box, "you always cry when it rains. Come on; let's get you out of those wet clothes."

We moved into Vira's bedroom. This was the only room of the apartment not decorated in chirpy fifties decor. Vira's bedroom walls were black, and her twin bed had a canopy of black lace and her windows were fitted with black lacy curtains. Everything was black and lace, basically, which gave the room a strange Victorian, haunted-dollhouse-type feel.

The one place I felt more at home than home and Vira's kitchen was Vira's bedroom.

Vira rummaged around in her closet, and I stripped while her back was turned. She tossed a fluffy black robe over her shoulder. It smelled like rosewater and lemons as I slipped it on.

I moved to sit on the bed but was greeted by a furious yowl from something moving underneath the blankets.

"Careful!" Vira shouted, diving over to the bed to pull a little bundle of fur out from under my butt.

"What *is* that? And what was it doing under your sheets?"

"My cat! Rain. Don't you remember? She likes to sleep under the blankets." She presented the kitten to me proudly. Rain was scrawny and twisty and very, very cute. "When she dies—in, like, eighteen years—I think I'll have Mom turn her into a lamp."

I scratched Rain between the ears. "May you live a long and happy life."

Vira put the kitten down, and Rain burrowed herself underneath the covers of the bed again. Vira pushed her to one side, lit some tall white pillar candles in her defunct fireplace, and then we sat across from each other on the bed.

"I'm so sorry all this is happening to you," she said.

"Ain't no thing," I said, but we both knew that it *was* a thing, and that it was a thing that really sucked.

"I know why you came here," Vira said.

"Because I love you and I missed you and I wanted to spend time with someone who doesn't think I did something to Annabella?"

"Nope. Because you want to solve a murder and you know the best way to start—"

"Oh no."

"—is by contacting the spirit world and giving them a quick *hello, how do you do?*"

I groaned. Vira slid off the bed and crossed the room to her closet, standing on tiptoes to pull something down from the top shelf.

Vira's Ouija board was made of wood the color of stained tea, and it said *Talking Board* across the top in curved letters. The word *yes* was written in the top left corner, the word *no* was written in the top right. At the bottom: *Good-bye.* The middle of the board held the alphabet and the numbers, zero through ten. The planchette was cool when Vira placed it into my hands. She set the board on the bed and arranged it just so between us. Then she sat down again and looked at me expectantly.

"You know how I feel about this," I said.

How I felt about it: very creepy.

I wasn't entirely convinced that the spirit world was so easily accessible that an old wooden board would suffice to serve as mediator between this plane of existence and theirs, but if that *were* the case, I also wasn't entirely convinced that was a good thing to play around with. And I didn't know what sort of spirits would be so eager to talk to two teenaged girls sitting on a flooded island in the middle of a rainstorm, anyway, but I couldn't imagine it would be the good ones.

"What do you intend to accomplish here?" she asked,

even though technically this wasn't even my idea. But I knew intentions were important. Especially when it came to creepy things like Ouija boards. Intentions were everything.

"I want to ask about Annabella's killer," I said. "Who killed Annabella? And where was my sister the night it happened?"

She took my hand and maneuvered it and the planchette onto the board.

I suddenly didn't feel well; my belly ached with some vague discomfort and my palms felt a little sweaty.

"Vira?"

"I'm concentrating."

The room felt suddenly warmer, like the candles were throwing off more heat than their tiny flames would suggest.

"Vira, is something happening?"

"Who killed Annabella?" Vira said, but she wasn't talking to me, she was directing her words toward the board between us. We both had the tips of our fingers on the planchette and the absolute scariest part of how it jumped into motion is that I knew Vira would never, ever push it. She took this shit way too seriously.

"That's not me, that's not me," I said.

"I know, shush," Vira said. She looked positively radiant, alive with excitement.

The planchette moved to point at the letter *E*.

The planchette moved to point at the letter *V.*

I wished desperately that it would spell out something non–sinister and light, like how about: *E-V-entually the rain will stop and Annabella's death was just a joke, she's actually fine and well and also you guys are totally safe and everything is great!!!!!!*

The planchette moved to point at the letter *I.*

The planchette moved to point at the letter *L.*

Evil.

Of course the planchette spelled out the word *evil*, because life could never be calm and easy, life always had to be scary and dangerous and mean. The planchette kept moving.

The planchette moved to point at the letter *M.*

The planchette moved to point at the letter *A.*

The planchette moved to point at the letter *N.*

The planchette stopped moving.

"Evil man," Vira said, mostly to herself, but also, I thought, because she considered the phrase *evil man* to be too good and creepy not to say out loud. "Do you know his name?"

The planchette moved to point at the word *no.*

"Hmm," Vira said.

"I'm going to pee myself," I whispered.

"At least we've ruled out some genders," Vira said, choosing to ignore me. "Of course it's a fucking *man*. Men are always killing things. Okay. Where was Mary Fernweh the night Annabella was murdered?"

The planchette moved to point at the letter *W*.

The planchette moved to point at the letter *I*.

The planchette moved to point at the letter *T*.

The planchette moved to point at the letter *H*.

The planchette moved to point at the letter *H*.

The planchette moved to point at the letter *E*.

The planchette moved to point at the letter *R*.

And then, as if it wanted to be very clear that it would share no more knowledge with us, the planchette moved to point at the word *good-bye*.

Vira didn't look up from the board. She let her fingers fall away, but she just stared at the planchette like it was going to do something. For its part, the planchette sat motionless on the board, like a completely innocent thing. I thought the silence in the room was going to kill me but as soon as I opened my mouth to speak, Vira held a finger up. *Shush*.

Then she said, "With her. The planchette spelled—"

"I know—"

"With her." She finally looked up at me. She looked more confused than anything, like she was trying to wrap her brain around what we'd just learned. "Do you remember what I said? Maybe I wasn't specific enough? We don't know who the *her* is."

"Vira, I think if we can be confident about anything in this world, it's that you know how to be specific with your Ouija questions."

Vira put her hand to her mouth and bit one nail, almost methodically. She shook her head a little. "And Mary told you—"

"That she didn't do it. Yeah."

"So if she didn't do it—"

"Then why is this thing saying she did?" I finished.

Vira shook her head again. "Well, it's not saying she *did* do it. It's just saying . . . she was there, maybe? Or maybe she saw Annabella before? Honestly it would be really nice of the spirit realm if we could get another question or two," she said, and poked the planchette for emphasis. Nothing happened.

"Well, I guess we've figured one thing out," I said after a minute.

"What?" Vira asked, her voice barely a whisper.

"There's a whole lot my sister isn't telling me."

So maybe Billy Kent had a reason to be wary of us, after all.

Maybe everybody did.

I cut through the graveyard on the way home. Autumnal, eternal, welcoming. The rain here was not as fierce; it died down to a steady, light trickle. The ground was soggy with wet leaves. Although it must have been after midnight by that point, the moon was bright in the sky and lit everything with a soft, yellow glow.

Vira had given me dry clothes to wear (black jeans,

black turtleneck, black lacy bra) but those, too, were already damp. I propped the umbrella up against a grave and sat down on a stone bench. Because I couldn't go home, because I couldn't think of *where* to go, so I figured I might as well stay there and make myself comfortable.

Vira had given me a spoon and a pint of Broken Hearts ice cream for the road, which seemed appropriate. I pulled the top off the carton and started eating. It was that perfect temperature: soft and creamy, not too melty. I was halfway through the pint when I heard the whistling, and somehow, though I didn't think I'd heard him whistle before, I knew who it was.

Harrison Lowry.

He hadn't seen me yet, and so I was gifted the rare pleasure of watching the movements of someone who thinks he's completely alone. Harrison whistled a somber, depressing tune that sounded a little bit like the By-the-Sea shanty. He walked with his hands in the pockets of his trench coat, which was just a little too big for him, in an adorable sort of way, in a way that made him seem a little younger than he was. His hair was wet and messy, and he didn't have an umbrella with him. And he looked sad, distant—like he was in another world entirely. That was probably why he hadn't noticed me yet, although he'd come to rest not ten feet away from me.

Not knowing what else to do, I cleared my throat.

Harrison jumped a mile, and then he saw me and smiled

and put a hand over his heart. "Geez Louise," he said, adding "geez Louise" to the list of things that made Harrison Lowry strangely appealing. "Georgina! What a strange place to meet."

I felt an overwhelming happiness—that he didn't run away the moment he saw me, that he didn't seem that bothered at all to be so close to me, and that he even seemed, maybe, pleased to have run into me. I held the ice cream out to him, and he came and sat next to me on the bench and took it.

"Tell me," he said, taking a bite of Broken Hearts, "what brings you to the graveyard in the middle of this rainy night?"

"I didn't have anywhere else to go," I said. "You?"

"A little bit of insomnia, I'm afraid. I spent so many nights looking for Annabella that now I can't seem to sleep. I didn't want to wake my sister, what with all my tossing and turning."

Ah, Prue.

Her name still sent a little rush of warmth down my arms, even though I hadn't seen her since the funeral. It was nice to know that she was well, even in the chaos of everything.

Harrison chuckled, took another bite of ice cream. "I bet it gets old, dealing with all these bird lovers, doesn't it?" he said after a minute. "I think we're all prone to the sentimental. Even those of us who didn't know her well."

"It doesn't get old," I said softly. "It's nice. What made you want to find her in the first place?"

"Just the idea, I think, of seeing something that so few people before me have seen . . . It became a bit of an obsession. My sister would say it's a *big* obsession, I'm sure."

"It's nice that you have each other," I said.

"It's nice to have sisters, isn't it? You would know," he said, and looked at me out of the very corner of his eye, like he was trying to hide how eager he was to hear my response. Like he had heard something.

"I do have one of those, yeah."

"It's nice," he repeated. He looked so suddenly sad, sitting there, and more like a little kid than ever, his shoulders hunched and his arms hugged around his knees and every inch of him completely dripping wet.

"I'm glad you don't hate me," I blurted out. I wished I could pluck the words out of the air and force them back in my mouth, back down my throat. But you can't unsay things once they're out in the world. Not even Fernweh women can manage that.

Harrison swallowed. He put the pint on the bench between us, resting the spoon carefully across its top. "How do I put this," he wondered aloud. "All right. Georgina, I don't believe for a second that your sister—or anyone in your family, for that matter—had anything to do with Annabella's death."

"How come?" I asked.

I really needed to learn how to keep my mouth shut unless it was to say *thank you for not thinking we're murderers*.

"You're all smart women," Harrison said. "And it would be decidedly *un*smart to sabotage your only means of livelihood."

"We wouldn't kill the bird because without the bird there won't be any birdheads, and without the birdheads there would be nobody to stay at the inn," I translated.

"Exactly."

"How come you're the only one intelligent enough to figure that out?" I asked, even though I was thinking something more along the lines of *you don't know my sister; her motivations are a little harder to pinpoint*.

"I've been thinking about that," Harrison said, picking the ice cream up again, taking a thoughtful bite. "And I think it's because we're the newbies."

The word *newbies* coming out of Harrison Lowry's mouth made me laugh out loud. He smirked in response.

"I just mean," he continued, "that of all the birdheads here, I'm the most removed. I've never been to By-the-Sea, I've never met you or your sister before this summer. I don't have a real attachment to you yet. No offense."

"None taken." The ice cream was exchanged from Harrison's hand to mine. A symbiotic ice cream relationship in a graveyard. One could do worse.

"There's a lot of emotion running around. The birdheads just want to blame somebody and get it over with.

And with all the rumors floating around about your family already, I think it makes sense they've chosen Mary as their scapegoat."

"Not rumors," I said. I suddenly didn't care much about the Fernweh family secrecy. It hadn't gotten us anywhere but suspicious looks and whispered accusations.

"Not rumors," Harrison repeated.

"If you're referring to the general spookiness of the Fernweh women then no, not rumors," I clarified.

"Spookiness."

"You know. Boil and bubble and all that."

"Ah. Well, I guess that changes things a little."

"Oh?"

"Back to the drawing board. No telling what you may or may not have done."

But he was smiling. And there was also an earnestness there, like he was taking my magicky revelation at face value. That was sort of nice.

"Have you ever heard that poem?" he asked, suddenly distant, looking past me.

"What poem?"

The ice cream was almost gone.

"'In her tomb by the sounding sea,'" Harrison said.

"Ah. Of course I've heard that poem. Poe was quite taken with the theme of death."

"Of women in particular. Sort of morbid, no?"

"What about it?"

"Hmm? Well, it's been in my head since I stepped off the ferry. I never considered myself much of a poetry person."

"Well. Islands. The sea. Rain. Graveyards. Dead things. It's hard not to feel poetic here."

"I think you have a point."

"Harrison—will you take a walk with me?" I asked.

That declaration on the widow's walk buzzed around in my head, loud and angry, *I will find who did this*. Even if that person might be my sister.

"Where?" Harrison asked.

"To somewhere unpleasant."

"Ah," he said. "I am at your disposal."

And we began to walk.

The entrance to the Elmhursts' barn was roped off by bright-yellow police tape. It was raining in earnest over here, just a short walk from the graveyard. We huddled underneath my one umbrella as Harrison fiddled with the lock on the door, wiggling a paper clip around inside it until it popped open with a soft *click*. He let it fall into his hand and then, looking around to make sure no one had seen us, we ducked into the dark mouth of the barn.

Harrison pulled a flashlight out of the pocket of his trench coat (where he'd also pulled the paper clip from, which begged the question: what *else* did he have in there?) and clicked it on. I put the umbrella near the door to dry out.

"What exactly are we doing here?" he asked.

"Didn't you know? We're solving a murder," I said. I grabbed the flashlight from him and put it under my chin.

"And what do you expect to find here?" he asked.

I handed the flashlight back to him. "Something the police missed."

"When you say *the police* like that, it implies more than just a sheriff and a deputy," Harrison said. "It's sort of false advertising."

"Fair."

He scanned his flashlight around the interior of the barn. "There's an overhead light in here somewhere, isn't there?"

I found the light switch on the wall and turned it on. The barn was washed in pale, dusty light. I half expected there to be a bird-shaped white chalk outline in the dirt marking where Annabella was found, but the ground was clear. The nest was gone. It looked like nothing out of the ordinary had ever happened here.

"I don't even know what I'm looking for," I admitted.

Harrison tossed the flashlight from hand to hand. He looked around the barn. "So far we don't seem to be showing much promise as sleuths."

"I know." I took a deep breath. "All right. You take the loft. I'll look around down here. Shout if you see anything."

So Harrison climbed carefully up the wooden ladder that led to the lofted area, and I explored the ground floor, the wood underneath my feet creaking as I walked around. I had "Annabel Lee" stuck in my head now, and I kept seeing shadows moving out of the corner of my eye because the half-light made everything spookier than it was.

Then Harrison started whistling again, and *that* made everything spookier than it was, too, and so finally, my nerves shot to hell and my skin crawling with goose bumps, I climbed up the ladder to meet Harrison in the loft. Because I didn't want to be alone. Because the phrase *higher ground* was suddenly ringing in my ears. Because outside the rain beat a torrential staccato against the roof, and I thought my heartbeat might be trying to match it.

It was brighter up here (closer to the overhead lamps), and I felt instantly more relaxed. I forced myself to breathe, breathe, breathing through the panic I could feel welling up in my chest. A sort of buzzing around my rib cage. The ever-familiar feeling of fear.

"Harrison?"

He turned around to face me, and as he did, the beam of his flashlight caught on something by his foot. A flash of gold. I bent down to pick it up and held it in my cupped hands. I felt that icy trickle of horror when you are home alone and hear a sound too loud to be just the house settling, or when you are walking at night and suddenly hear footsteps following too closely behind you.

It was my sister's necklace.

I would know it anywhere. It was a delicate heart-shaped locket, identical to the one given to me on our sixteenth birthday. Matching lockets. Mary wore hers often; mine was tucked safely inside the top drawer of my bureau. I'd never been one for jewelry.

The Ouija board had said: *with her.*

And now I had proof of it: Mary was here, in the barn, the night Annabella was murdered.

I knew if I opened this locket I would find a picture of the two of us on one side—Mary and me—and a picture of my mother and father on the other.

The clasp of the necklace was broken.

I held it up to Harrison, so he could see it. "It's my sister's."

"What would your sister's locket be doing in this barn?" Harrison asked, his voice careful and measured, like he was trying to keep something out of it.

"I know she didn't kill Annabella," I said, but even as the words left my mouth I wondered—did I really know that? It was my sister's word against the Ouija board, against this locket. It was my sister's word against everything piling up against it.

"But if she was here, she must know something," Harrison said. "Have you asked her?"

I shook my head. "I don't know what she knows. She's being . . . strange."

"Strange," Harrison repeated.

"Oh, please don't change your mind about us," I said quickly.

"Not changing my mind. Just . . . processing."

"Did you find anything else up here?"

"Feathers," Harrison said.

I took a step closer to him. "What?"

"Feathers," he repeated. "But not Annabella's."

"Not Annabella's."

"Look."

He took one step to the side, revealing a small, neat pile of feathers. They were white and long and clean. Not Annabella's.

"What kind of bird did these come from?" I asked.

I felt sick to my stomach.

"It's hard to say," Harrison said. "They don't look familiar to me."

"I think I need some air," I said.

"Mmm," Harrison said. He picked up a feather and carefully put it into a pocket of his trench coat.

I wondered again what else he might have in those pockets. The reason why it was raining so much? The location of my missing magic powers? That which my sister refused to tell me? The identity of the evil man who'd killed Annabella? What part my sister must have played in her death?

My head was spinning.

I descended the ladder quickly and raced across the barn to the door, which was standing ajar just an inch or so. I pushed out into the cold, wet evening. The moon was fat and almost full in the sky above me. I leaned against the outside wall of the barn and breathed and breathed and breathed.

Until I heard the barn door creak open and closed, and I felt a hand on my shoulder.

I opened my eyes.

Harrison, holding my umbrella.

"Are you all right?" he asked.

"Just needed a little air."

He offered me his arm. "Let's go home, shall we?"

I took it, gratefully.

And we set off into the dark.

That night, late, Mary crawled into my bed. I moved over to make room for her.

"I can't sleep," she said.

"Where did you go?"

"When?"

"At the party, Mary. Where did you go?"

"Oh. I just got there and I saw the lights and I heard all the people laughing, and I couldn't do it."

"You're cold."

"Can I stay in here?"

Usually it was cramped with the two of us in one bed,

but tonight Mary felt smaller, like she took up less space.

"Of course."

"Did you have fun? At the party?" she asked.

"I didn't stay either. Why are you so cold?"

"I don't know," Mary said.

I reached down to the foot of the bed and found the extra quilt that was folded there. I draped it over her, tucking it under her chin.

I knew I should have told her about the Ouija board, about finding her necklace in the barn, but I couldn't. She was shaking she was so cold, and I couldn't make myself ask her why she had lied to me. I couldn't make myself ask her what had really happened.

The bed felt so much colder with my sister's shivering body next to mine. I moved an inch away from her.

"Stop that," she said. "You're my *sister*."

When she said that word it felt more like a curse than a familial relation.

I took her hand in mine, and my fingers froze to ice.

"Mary?"

"Not now," she said.

When I woke up, she was gone.

In her place: plain white feathers.

FEATHERS

The next morning I picked white feathers off my white sheets and stuck them into a white pillowcase I'd taken off one of my pillows. My mother came in when it was halfway full.

"What's all this about?" she asked.

"I think something's going on with Mary."

My mother picked up a feather and held it between her thumb and her middle finger. She looked at it. She smelled it. She licked it (gross).

"What are they?" I asked.

She sat down on the bed, causing a small swarm of feathers to rise up and float around her. She collected them in her lap, examining each one, twirling them around.

"I'm not sure," she said.

"Are they coming . . ."

"From your sister?" She exhaled slowly, thinking. She

looked very unmagicky today. I think, given everything, that was a deliberate choice. She wore faded baggy jeans and a white sleeveless collared shirt tucked into them. She had rainboots on and her hair was tied into a ponytail at her neck. I felt a sudden rush of emotion for her, this woman picking feathers from my bed and piling them into a careful mountain on top of her thighs.

"Your sister has had an emotional upset," she said finally. "We all have." That seemed to be putting it lightly. She opened her mouth to say more but paused, decided against it, dumped the feathers from her lap into the pillowcase. Then she sniffed. Once. Twice. "Georgina," she scolded. "You smell like cheap tricks."

"Oh, it was nothing—"

"The spirit world is not *nothing*!"

"I don't even believe in that stuff, really. It was all Vira's idea."

"Cheap tricks and hay," she amended. "What exactly are you up to?"

"Okay, well, we *did* use the Ouija board. But just a little," I admitted, sitting next to her on the bed.

"Did you learn anything?"

"The person who killed Annabella is a man," I said.

"It's always a man," she said grimly. "Anything else?"

If I wasn't ready to tell Mary that I knew she was in the barn the night Annabella was murdered, I certainly wasn't ready to tell my mom. I was suddenly thankful she had never fed us a truth serum (that I knew of) and did my best to make my face as neutral as possible.

"That's all. The spirits were pretty unforthcoming."

"And the hay?"

"What?"

"Why do you smell like hay, Georgina?"

"Oh."

"You went back to the barn."

"Just for a minute."

"And you found?"

"Nothing at all," I said. The locket burned in my bureau, announcing my lie, and I was afraid it would set the whole thing on fire. But my mother just nodded to herself.

"Throw those over the cliffs," she said, getting up, pointing to the bag of feathers. "Or bury them, or burn them, I don't care."

"But if they came from Mary, isn't that a little harsh?"

"If they came from Mary, I'm sure she'll just go ahead and make more," she said. She looked tired, strange, worn thin around the edges.

"You don't think this is like . . ." I paused. I held up a feather in the hopes that it could convey what I meant without me having to actually say it. That Mary wasn't the first Fernweh woman to leave feathers on her pillow when she woke up in the morning. That was how it started with Annabella too.

My mother sighed. "If it is," she began, "then it's your

sister's business. And I suppose, for now, we'll just have to wait and see."

"Mom, that's not helpful at all," I said.

She kissed the side of my head and let herself out of the room.

"That's not helpful at all!" I called after her.

She did not come back.

Among the small number of people not avoiding Fernwehs like the plague was Peter, who gladly obliged my request to get rid of the feathers. It felt like something much more illicit than it was, handing him the overstuffed pillowcase and relaying my mother's instructions to make it disappear.

I'd found him in the backyard, trying his best to sweep rainwater off the porch, and he wrinkled his nose as he peeked inside the case. "Feathers?" he asked.

"It's sort of a long story."

"All right," he said. "I'll take care of it now."

"Only not the pillowcase," I said. "I'd like that back."

"Sure thing, Georgina."

I watched him take the pillowcase around to the front of the house, and I was about to go inside when I heard a sharp whistle from the back door of the house. It was Harrison, but he shook his head when I went to meet him, and instead vanished and reappeared a few moments later at an open window. He made me sit in a wicker chair on the porch, and he hid himself behind the curtain.

"It's better like this," he said. "More undercover. If they think I hate you, they're more likely to talk to me. Let something slip."

"That sleuthing yesterday really went to your head, huh?"

"Look what I found," he hissed.

He held up a feather to the window screen. I stared at it for a long time and then he scolded me for being too obvious, so I looked back across the yard.

A feather.

But not a white feather.

He'd found one of Annabella's feathers.

"Where did you . . ."

"Don't be mad," he said.

"Where did you find it?"

"In your sister's room."

"What were you doing in my sister's room?" I hissed.

"I said don't be mad! I was just looking around. For clues." He paused. "Maybe that sleuthing *did* go to my head. Just a bit."

"And where exactly did you find it?"

He paused again. It was a heavy sort of pause. The kind that made my stomach twist in anticipation. "In her nightstand," he finally said.

My stomach twisted again. "Her nightstand?"

"Look, Georgina, I still don't think your sister did it, but obviously she knows something. And she's an easy target;

public opinion weighs heavily here, and as far as they're all concerned, she's as good as tried. Which, if true, makes it very lucky that I went snooping and found this before somebody else did, so you should go ahead and forgive me for that."

"I'll take it into consideration."

"Also . . . ," he said, rather uncomfortably, with a little less bravado in his voice than just a moment ago.

"What?"

"Have you considered . . . You know. The *actual* legal implications here?"

"What legal implications?"

"Animal cruelty. Does By-the-Sea have a judge?"

"Of course By-the-Sea has a judge."

Eleanora Avery.

I was unsure whether she'd actually ever tried a case or not.

"You don't think they'll take her to court, do you?" I asked.

"This is your island," Harrison replied. "You tell me."

This was my island, all right.

Where nothing ever happened.

Where people loved a good drama.

"Give me that feather," I said.

I took the feather up to the widow's walk, where I knew I'd be alone, where I knew no other guest would find me.

I carried an umbrella and a large jar candle up to the roof and was surprised to find my sister already there, almost like she was waiting for me. She wore a long white dress that blew wildly in the breeze.

"The island's flooding," Mary said, not turning around. "Have you noticed?"

She was right. Bottle Hill rose gently above the shallow pond that surrounded it. An island on a bigger island. The rain fell in a loud roar. It sounded like static turned up high on a broken television set.

My sister had feathers in her hair.

Every so often one would dislodge and float away on the manic breeze, sailing rockily on the wind until it succumbed to the rain and drowned.

"Mary, where the fuck are these coming from?" I asked, my voice frantic. I picked one off her shoulder.

"Hmm? Oh. I'm not sure," she said. She plucked the feather from my fingers and considered it. She smelled it, exactly like my mother had. That must be some instinct lost to me, the non-magical Fernweh. I had no desire to smell the feathers falling from my sister's hair. I already knew they'd smell like the whole island. The salt. The magic. And now: the rain.

"Harrison found this in your room," I said, and held out the single feather that was unmistakable in its origin.

"What was he doing in there?" she said sharply.

It was hard to describe how my sister looked. Smaller.

Scared. But more than that—like something was missing. Like something had been taken from her. But I had no idea what that could be. Comfort? Safety? All of the above?

"I was going to burn it." I showed her the candle, to demonstrate. "Mary, where did it *come* from? If somebody else had found this . . ."

"They already think I did it. It's not like having proof would change anything."

"So this is proof?"

"I didn't do it," she snapped, and for a moment, there she was: my sister, the bitch in all her glory, long hair whipping about her face, her feet leaving the floor of the widow's walk to hover an inch above it. I could have hugged her. And I would have, if at that moment a strong gust of wind hadn't ripped the feather from my fingers, sending it floating in a vicious cyclone down to the backyard . . .

In front of the waiting eyes of two of the birdheads—Hep and Lucille—who were sharing the same umbrella as they took a stroll around the yard.

"Mary, get *down*!" I yelled, and yanked her to her feet so hard that she fell to her knees.

So when Hep and Lucille turned as one to look up at the house to see where the feather—Annabella's feather—had come from—

All they saw was me.

At that point, it seemed like there was only one thing to do.

I was used to cleaning up my sister's messes. I was used to taking the blame.

So I raised my hand—

and waved.

Blame shifted from my sister to me as easily as a feather caught on a strong breeze.

It didn't bother me at all.

I considered a lifetime of living with Mary, of cleaning up after all of her messes, big and small, to be practice for this. I held my head high and looked every birdhead I passed in the eye. I walked with my shoulders back and a jaunt in my step that I hope conveyed the message: *Don't bother fucking with me. You won't get very far.*

I tried to pretend that I thought my sister was innocent.

I tried to pretend that I didn't think about Clarice Fernweh and her two locked-away children almost every minute of every day.

I tried to keep my promise to Annabella: *I will find who did this.*

That promise seeped into my dreams.

I was in the barn again, only this time it was filled with water, and this time my sister was drowning. I woke up choking, terrified, and I went to see Harrison that evening—to inform him of my renewed sense of purpose, my rekindled desire to clear not only my sister's name but now mine as well.

And I was genuinely surprised when Prue answered.

With everything going on, Prudence Lowry had been mostly removed from the forefront of my mind. But now, standing before me in a simple striped cotton dress, her mouth opened in surprise, her hands holding what smelled like a cup of peppermint tea, I felt a rush of affection, a rush of hope, and a rush of . . .

Something else. Because Prue wasn't looking like she was that happy to see me. In fact—it was kind of the exact opposite.

I felt my heart sink to somewhere around my stomach as it occurred to me that Prue might be of the same mind-set as most of the island: that the Fernweh women had something to do with Annabella's death.

"I was just looking for your brother," I said quickly, feeling my face grow hot as Prue continued to stare at me in a way I could not begin to discern. "If he's not here, I can go."

"What? No, you don't have to—he's not here, no, but you should come in," Prue said, shaking her head, moving aside for me.

"I can just come back later," I said, turning around. I felt her hand close softly around my upper arm, and I hated myself for noting how warm it was.

"Is something wrong?" she asked.

I turned around again. "Do you think my sister killed Annabella?"

Prue looked confused. She removed her hand (*put it back, put it back*) and took a step away from the door. "Can you come in for a second?"

"I don't know," I said. But I didn't move.

"There's something I've been wanting to talk to you about," Prue said quietly. She gestured into the room. Two twin beds, one made neatly and one made messily, with clothes scattered across the quilt and a straw hat on the pillow.

I stepped inside and closed the door behind me.

Prue sat on her bed (the messy one, which made my heart soar with I didn't even know what) and gestured to the other. Harrison's, perfectly made with not an inch of fabric mussed. Figured.

We sat across from each other. Prue still held that mug in her hands, so tightly that her knuckles were turning white.

Then she laughed. "Okay, I definitely don't think your sister had anything to do with this," she said. "Sorry, that actually . . . I wasn't expecting that."

"Oh. Really?"

"Really. Promise. The thought never crossed my mind."

I felt a welcome rush of relief and relaxed a little on the bed. "Okay. That's good. That's great." But Prue still looked a little . . . strange. "Is there something else?"

"There isn't really an easy way to say this," she said.

"Prue? Whatever it is . . ."

She stifled a yawn, and I noticed how tired she looked. Her mascara was smudged a little underneath her eyes; her hair hadn't been washed in a few days. Her dress was wrinkled. She looked like she hadn't slept either. I remembered the time, a few summers ago, when Hep Shackman had stayed up for forty-eight hours taking notes on Annabella's nesting habits. He'd become convinced that he, too, was a bird, and Annabella's eggs weren't hatching because he was the one who was supposed to sit on them. My mother had given him a cup of tainted tea and he hadn't come out of his room for a day and a night. When he finally did, he had to admit that he was not, in fact, a bird, and that sitting on eggs would do nothing more than crush them. There was something about Prue now that reminded me of that—maybe the way her eyes seemed to take a few extra seconds to focus, the way she kept gripping that mug in her hands.

Finally she took a deep breath, set her mug on the nightstand, and said, "I think I've been avoiding you. Just a little bit. But not because of Annabella, it's nothing like that. It's just . . . you're the first girl I've ever kissed. And I didn't know how to tell you that."

"Oh," I said. "Wow."

"I mean, I know I'm . . . I know I like girls. And guys. The girl thing is sort of newer. Harrison is the only one who knows."

"Oh," I said again. And for good measure: "Wow."

"I know kissing you shouldn't have thrown me as much

as it did, and that's not even the right word for it, really, it just sort of . . . it sort of made everything real. Like a confirmation of everything I thought I was feeling." She was pulling on her fingers, bending them back. "And then with everything that happened . . . I just haven't been getting that much sleep."

"You're not alone."

"So I was avoiding you, yes. Not because I thought your sister killed Annabella, God. No, I was avoiding you because it was easier than having to process what it means to have kissed a girl. And I'm sorry, I just couldn't . . . I didn't know what to do. After that night . . . I mean, we kissed, it was this huge moment for me, and then my brother totally interrupted it, and then the next morning . . ."

"Kind of killed the vibe," I said.

"I'm sorry. It's just been . . . a lot."

"Well, we don't have to . . . I mean, that could be it. We could just forget it ever happened."

"I don't want to do that either," Prue said, so quietly that her words were almost blown away. I had to catch them in my hands, bring them to my ears, strain to decipher what exactly it was that she meant.

"Me neither," I said.

"I like you. Like, I *really* like you. I'm sorry this is so hard for me."

"Whatever you need," I said. "However slow or fast or whatever. Anything is fine with me."

And I meant it.

It had been easy for me; I'd been born into a long family of women who didn't give a single hoot about who you chose to love. I'd known I was gay since I was six years old, when I'd fallen in complete and all-encompassing love with my kindergarten teacher, Miss Farid. I was twelve when I told my mother I was gay, and it had been like asking her to pass the coffeepot. She'd only been so happy to lend her blessing. Mary had been equally easy; she'd rolled her eyes, said "Duh," and remarked that it was a relief she didn't have to compete with me for guys, even though, she was quick to point out, I wouldn't have been much competition.

Vira was the easiest of all. I told her I liked girls. She told me she didn't like anyone, at least not in a sexual way. We breathed huge sighs of relief and that was that.

So I had absolutely no idea what it might be like to contemplate your sexuality under anything less than ideal conditions. I had no idea what things were like for Prue at home, what the rest of her family and friends were like. Did her friends know? What was it like to be Prue at that moment, quiet and thoughtful, her fingers tapping out some foreign rhythm on the bed. I wanted to hold her hand, to quiet the impulses that made it impossible for her to sit still, but I didn't want to disrespect whatever music she heard.

I couldn't remember whose turn it was to speak, so I

finally said, "How long have you known?"

"That I like girls too? About a year."

"What happened?" I asked.

Prue blushed a little. "I was at a coffee shop with my friend. There was this piano player, a woman . . ." She paused. "There have been a few others since then. And you, of course. You sort of confirmed things."

I was very close to getting up the nerve to close the space between us and possibly kiss her again when the door to the room flew open and Harrison raced inside. He was soaking wet, and he started talking to me like it didn't surprise him in the least that I was there, that he'd maybe even been expecting me.

"You have to come with me. Right away. No time to waste. Put some shoes on. Quick as you can."

"What's going on?" I asked.

"Your sister has climbed a very big tree, and she's threatening to jump."

I was torn.

On the one hand, Mary wasn't in any real danger. She'd jumped and/or fallen out of plenty of trees before (the ability to float didn't necessarily go hand in hand with the ability to keep one's balance) and she just drifted lazily down to the ground, landing on the grass with a gentle bump that didn't so much as bruise her skin.

On the other hand, Harrison and Prue didn't know

about Mary's gift. I guess I *had* told Harrison, more or less, that we had magic, but he didn't know what kind, and as far as I knew, Prue was still out of the loop. And while my mother had never sat me down to explicitly forbid me from spilling the beans, it was also sort of just known.

People knew we had magic.

It wasn't spoken of.

But this felt like a new By-the-Sea—one untethered from the rules of time and space, one floating higgledy-piggledy on an ocean that kept tossing it this way and that—and I couldn't for the life of me figure out my best course of action. And I hadn't even yet taken into account *why* my sister might have climbed the tallest tree on the island and was now threatening to jump off it. That was a mystery all on its own.

"And you're absolutely sure no one else saw her?" I asked Harrison, for the eighth or ninth or twentieth time.

"She's pretty hidden. You know. By leaves. Rain," he said. He was out of breath due to running full speed back to the inn and now, running back. "I'd just stopped under the tree for a bit of shelter. And then she called down to me, 'Hi, Harrison! Just wanted to warn you that I'm going to be jumping soon. Didn't want to startle you.'"

"That's all she said?"

"That's all she said."

"Does your sister have a history of jumping out of trees?" Prue asked.

"Well . . . ," I said.

"Well?" Prue repeated.

"Okay." I stopped running. Harrison and Prue stopped too, and we all huddled underneath an umbrella that wasn't even a rain umbrella at all, but a beach umbrella that somehow belonged to Prue, because of course Prue owned an enormous yellow-and-white-striped beach umbrella and had casually packed it for summer vacation. It felt a little bit like we were inside a tent. "I have something to tell you."

Prue and Harrison were rapt listeners. They both seemed to have guessed that I was about to drop something important on them.

"Right. So. All the rumors. The boil and bubble stuff," I said, repeating the phrase I'd used in the graveyard with Harrison. "All that's true, okay?"

I tried to gauge Prue's reaction without being too obvious about it. She was nodding her head, and when I looked at her she said, "Harrison told me."

"I hope that's okay," Harrison said quickly. "We don't have many secrets."

"I know what it's like having a sibling. I'm glad you told her," I replied. "So, going along with that whole thing . . . Mary can float."

"Fly?" Harrison exclaimed.

"She might use the word *fly*; the word *float* is a tad more accurate," I clarified.

"Wow," Prue said. "So she *does* have a history of jumping out of trees."

"No. I mean, not really. This is new. She knows . . . we don't use our powers . . . I mean, she doesn't use her powers in front of other people. It's not how it works."

"What can *you* do?" Prue asked.

"I'm a dud," I said quickly, in the vein of pulling a sticky bandage off a wound in one unthinking breath. It felt like I was admitting something not only to them, but to myself. We were almost eighteen, and it was time I came to terms with it: I wasn't getting any powers.

"What do you mean?" Harrison asked.

"I'm just normal. I'm just a sidekick."

I started running again, forgoing the relative dryness of Prue's umbrella for the chance to move faster. As a result, I reached the tree before either of them. And I also reached the tree soaking wet.

The impressive canopy *did* provide fairly adequate cover from the storm. I found Mary immediately, looking strange and languid, sitting far up in the tree with her back against the trunk and her legs spread out on a branch and crossed at the ankles.

"Mary?" I called up to her.

She didn't look like herself. Her dress was too big, her hair was too messy. When she looked down at me, I could have sworn her eyes flashed black.

"Hi, Georgie," she said.

"Can you come down?"

"I kind of like it up here."

"You told Harrison you were going to jump."

"I don't think I'm ready to jump quite yet."

"You know I don't love heights."

"You don't have to do anything you don't want to do."

But alas, the rules of sisterhood: if your sister took residence in the boughs of a tree, you were obligated to go and visit.

I rubbed my palms against my clothes, drying them.

"I'm not great at climbing trees," I said to Prue, who'd appeared beside me.

"And just to be clear, if you fall, you won't float?" she asked.

"Sink like a stone," I confirmed.

"Be careful," she said.

I started to climb. A few feet up I realized I'd blown a perfectly good opportunity for a tearful farewell kiss, but it was too late to go back and rectify that. I concentrated on the task at hand.

Mary watched me with some interest, but she didn't offer any tree-climbing tips. It was just as well. I didn't think I could listen to tips while at the same time not plummeting to my death.

Luckily, the tree was fairly easy to climb, offering many sturdy branches at very manageable intervals. I was on level with Mary after only a few minutes. I immediately made the mistake of looking down.

She put a hand on my arm to steady me.

Her fingers felt like feathers, but when I looked at them, they were just fingers.

"What the fuck are you doing up here?" I asked.

"I woke up this morning and I thought to myself, I suppose I'll go climb a tree," Mary said, shrugging, like it was perhaps the most normal thing in the world for young women to spend their free time in the branches of big trees.

"'I suppose I'll go climb a tree'? Nobody talks like that, Mary."

"My legs hurt. From walking."

"So you thought you'd give them a rest *in a tree*?"

"It's not as weird as you're making it sound."

"It feels pretty weird. Harrison and Prue think it's pretty weird."

Suddenly nervous, Mary asked, "They didn't tell anyone else where I was, right?"

"I don't think so. I mean, no—Harrison came to get me."

"Okay. You're sure?"

"Who else would he tell?"

"I just don't want anybody to know where I am." She frowned and rubbed her fingers against her temples, like she had a headache. Her eyes, her mouth, her jaw, her shoulders . . . everything looked smaller. Was something wrong with my eyes?

"Are you hiding from someone?" I asked.

"Evil man," she said, and I tried to remember if I'd told my sister what the Ouija board had said.

And then something clicked.

"You were in the barn with him," I said. "You didn't kill Annabella, but you know you did."

"It's not fair to read minds," Mary said, squinting. "Is that your thing?"

"No, it's not my thing, I—I found your necklace. In the loft."

Mary's face clouded over and for just a moment I saw something dark and broken there.

"Mary, what were you doing in the barn?"

"Gathering eggs," she said after a long minute. Then she smiled. "Do you want to know where they are? I'll tell you, but you have to promise not to tell anyone else where I am, okay? I'm safe here."

"Eggs? You have her eggs?"

She nodded and ran a hand through her hair, sending a small cascade of feathers down over the bough of the tree, down to where Harrison and Prue waited patiently below.

"I took them," she said. "To keep them safe."

"To keep them safe? From what?"

"If a man is angry enough to break a bird into a million pieces, what do you think he could do with her eggs?"

"Where are they?"

"In my bedroom. Under that floorboard in my closet."

She wiped at her cheeks as if she were crying, but her eyes were dry. "Eggs are so fragile, Georgina."

Around us the tree swayed gently in the breeze and a few drops of rain were blown into Mary's safe haven. She put her hand in her hair and pulled out one feather. It wasn't white anymore. They were getting darker.

"Who killed her?" I asked.

She made a motion, and I held my hands out flat as she placed a feather in my palm.

But just like the other feather on the widow's walk, this one only rested for a moment before it caught on a sudden gust—

And blew away.

And Mary leaned forward and whispered in my ear—

In a voice that sounded exactly like a birdsong—

In a voice that made it unavoidable, that thing I'd known for so long already—

My sister was turning into a bird.

And just like my namesake—the Georgina who came before me—there would be no magic I could use to save her.

III.

But our love it was stronger by far than the love
Of those who were older than we—
Of many far wiser than we—

once more from "Annabel Lee"
by Edgar Allan Poe

EVIL MAN

I realized halfway down the tree that our birthday was tomorrow.

In that post-Annabella world, it was hard to keep track of time. Days seemed to melt together. It could have been weeks that Mary and I were stuck up in that tree, weeks more before I reached the bottom and started walking back to the inn with Harrison and Prue.

The waters were so high that we were forced to overturn Prue's beach umbrella and use it as a makeshift boat. We paddled with our hands, ineffective scoops of water that propelled us forward at a snail's pace. The island was covered in water. The cliffs to our right had become a waterfall to the ocean. We steered clear of them; I didn't know if the magic would hold now or if we would plummet to our deaths below.

I told them about Mary.

"This is a strange island," Harrison said, dipping his hand into the new freshwater sea, as if to illustrate that not *only* was my sister turning into a bird, but we also had this flood to deal with.

"It's never been quite this strange," I said. "You missed many, many years of no floods and boring birdwatching and movie nights on the town green and uneventful summer solstices where hardly anyone even got naked."

"Yeah, but . . . there was still magic and stuff, right?" Prue pointed out.

"Super-boring magic. Honestly. We don't even own wands. Or pointy hats. It's nothing like it is in the movies. It's way more . . . normal."

"Normalcy is underrated," Harrison said.

When we got back to the inn, it smelled like vanilla and cinnamon; Aggie's island-famous birthday cake. The three of us—under better circumstances I might have called us something cute, like the three musketeers or the three amigos or the three stooges, but under these circumstances I couldn't bring myself to do so—stood in the kitchen and peered into the oven and watched an overlarge yellow circle rising to perfect golden perfection inside it.

"What's this for?" Prue asked.

"Tomorrow's our birthday," I said.

"Really?"

"Yup."

"Well, happy early birthday," Harrison said weakly.

We decided to break for a few minutes to change into dry clothes. It seemed like a losing battle; as soon as we stepped outside again we'd be waist-deep in water and any cute thoughts of being warm and not soaking would be far behind us. But still, for now, it felt nice to peel off my underwear and bra and pull on warmer clothes: jeans and a turtleneck I hadn't worn in five years at least, a heavy sweatshirt I used to wear to help my mother harvest herbs in the moonlight. I found thick wool socks and put them on under my rainboots. I piled my hair up into a bun on the top of my head. I wrapped a scarf around my neck and then I met the Lowrys outside Mary's room. We wanted to see the eggs, to make sure they were safe. Safe from what, I couldn't say.

Prue had pulled her hair into a wet ponytail; the back of her clean shirt was already damp where the end hit it.

The inn was strangely quiet. We hadn't run into a single birdhead on our way to the attic.

The door to Mary's bedroom was closed.

I wanted to know why my sister didn't feel safe and who she was hiding from up in that tree. When I'd asked her, when she'd leaned in to whisper to me, all she had said, all she'd repeated, was *evil man*.

"Well," Harrison said. "Should you do the honors?"

I reached out and gripped the doorknob with a hand that hopefully looked a lot sturdier than I felt, and then I twisted and pushed the door open.

It creaked a little, an appropriately creepy creak that made Prue cross her arms over her chest and made Harrison take a tiny, imperceptible step back. I took a big, steadying breath that didn't actually do anything to steady myself, and I stepped into the room and flicked the light switch on.

And of course nothing happened.

And of course then the hall lights winked out, and we were plunged into sudden, blinding darkness.

Prue grabbed my arm. Harrison shrieked. I reached back into Harrison's trench coat pocket (him wearing that trench coat indoors seemed very Harrison-appropriate) and pulled out the flashlight I knew would be there. I flicked it on just as a low rumble of thunder echoed through the house.

"It's the storm," I said. "It must have knocked out the power lines."

"It chose a most inconvenient moment to do so," Harrison pointed out.

My sister had candles scattered throughout her room. I found a book of matches in her nightstand drawer and went around lighting them. A massive bolt of lightning pierced the sky and lit up our faces in severe yellow. The roof was alive with the sound of rain. Harrison shut the door and locked it, then, after a moment's consideration, he pushed Mary's bureau in front of it.

"Can't really be too careful, can we?" he asked.

The candlelight caused a hundred different shadows to

come alive and dance across the walls of my sister's bedroom. I placed the flashlight on the bed and pointed it toward the closet. The door was shut.

I thought of the floorboard that lay within it, the one Mary had pried loose years ago; in its long history, it had hidden other such treasures as jewelry stolen from me, cookies stolen from Aggie, cinnamon whiskey stolen from our mother.

I thought back, but I didn't think it had ever held anything quite so precious as the last eggs Annabella would ever lay.

I opened the door.

Harrison and Prue stood sentry on either side of me as I knelt down and felt along the floor.

The loose board jiggled when my fingers ran across it. I forced my fingertips into the cracks between the boards and pulled upward. It popped up with ease.

And there, bundled in many of my sister's clean wool socks, were the eggs.

They were perfectly white, not a blemish on any of them.

I felt a rush of sadness for these eggs. They had no chance of hatching. A poor track record for their siblings combined with a lack of their mother's brooding left them no chance at all. They were cool to the touch and most likely already dead. I wanted to gather the pair of them in my hands and bring them over to a candle, warm them up and sing them to them and whisper to them and tell them stories of their mother and the legacy she had left behind. I wanted to wrap them in my sister's socks and tuck them into my pocket and walk around so, so carefully, as not to upset or disturb them in any way. I wanted to cuddle them and hide them and find out who'd killed their mom and do something terrible to him. Something to match the terribleness of what he'd done to Annabella.

"Georgina?" Prue said.

"They're here," I said.

And I left them alone, undisturbed, and stepped back so Prue and Harrison could have a look. Harrison had come all this way to see Annabella, so it felt right that at least he was able to see these eggs, perfect and eternal, although, for all intents and purposes, useless.

"They're beautiful," he said, and they honestly were. An entire lifeform self-contained in one smooth white sphere.

Prue left her brother and went to look out the window. "The waters are rising," she said.

We had dragged our boat-umbrella onto the porch, but now the porch was under a foot of water and the boat-umbrella was drifting languidly away, passengerless, a spot of bright against the dark blue of the rainwater.

"My sister was hiding from someone," I said, watching Harrison put the loose board back in its place and move a pair of Mary's shoes on top of it. If you didn't know exactly where to look, you'd have no idea two of Annabella's eggs were hidden there. "I think whoever killed Annabella might have done something to Mary."

"Done something?" Prue said. "Like what?"

"I don't know."

And when I didn't know something—like what sort of thing could happen to a girl to make her shrink and shrink and then ultimately, potentially, turn into a bird—there was one person who might.

Penelope Fernweh the Second.

The ladder to the widow's walk was folded into the ceiling, so I knew my mother wouldn't be up there. I went down to the kitchen, where Aggie was carefully icing the birthday cake. She quickly moved her body in front of it when she heard me at the door.

"I already saw," I said, smiling.

"Oh, the surprise is ruined," she said, and she went back to icing.

Aggie was a good cook, but she was an unreal cake maker. The yellow cake was completely covered by a smooth, creamy layer of buttery white frosting. She was working on the icing flowers now; there were at least twenty pastry bags spread around the counter, each holding a different shade of buttercream. There were delicate roses, vines that wound around the circumference of the cake, bright peonies, and yellow sunflowers.

"Aggie, it's beautiful," I said.

She set the icing bag on the counter and gathered me up in a hug. I realized it had been so long since I'd heard Aggie laugh. The kitchen felt empty without it.

"Your birthday snuck up on me this year," she whispered into my ear, then held me at arm's length to look at me. "It's been such a strange summer."

What would Aggie do now that Annabella was dead? If there were no birdheads to stay at the inn, if there were no birdheads to cook for . . .

I hugged her again, trying to imagine a summer where Aggie was not here, in this kitchen, every waking moment of the day. It felt impossible. When I finally pulled away from her, I could feel the tears in my eyes. She dabbed at my cheeks with her apron.

"I know," she said. "But everything is going to turn out all right."

I wanted to ask her how she knew that, how she could say that with even an ounce of conviction in her voice, but instead I shook my head, composing myself, and asked, "You haven't seen my mother anywhere, have you?"

"She's out back. In the rowboat. Have you seen the moon? I don't think I've ever seen the moon as full as it is tonight."

The back porch was under a foot of water, but my mother was waiting next to it in her rowboat, standing up, holding the railing for balance, like she had been waiting for me. Her hair was billowing all around her face in the breeze: long and brown and messy. I waded across the porch and stepped carefully into the rowboat. She sat down across from me and said, "This reminds me of the night you and your sister were born."

I had heard the story a million times, but I let her tell it to me again, and I listened like it was the very first time, because I loved to hear my mother speak.

She told me about the birth. About how I'd been her only child for five hours. About how I'd waited patiently with her to meet my sister. About how the rains had started the first time I'd cried.

"What are you doing out here?" I asked when she had finished talking.

She rowed the boat out into the backyard, navigating the floods with a deft hand. Somewhere near where the flower beds used to be, she stopped rowing. She raised the paddle above her head and then plunged it into the water like a spear, so it stuck into the wet earth below.

"Hold this, will you?" she said.

I took hold of the oar. I could feel the current underneath the water and the boat struggling against it. I held on tighter.

"What are you doing?" I asked again.

"The moon is good again. See?"

My mother lifted something from underneath her shirt: a tiny bottle she wore on a chain around her neck. I watched as she uncorked the bottle, smelled it, held it over the water and carefully poured it in.

The liquid inside was the color of sunshine. It smelled like leaves.

"What is that?" I asked.

"Your sister is hiding something," my mother said.

"You know?"

She nodded. "I found that loose floorboard when you were both eight. She hid a slice of cake inside it. I followed a trail of ants."

"The eggs are already cool," I said. "They must be dead."

My mother stood up and found her balance in the rocking boat. "*Nearly* dead," she said, and dove into the water in an elegant little arc. Her body made just the tiniest ripple as it disappeared beneath the surface.

She was gone for long enough that I got nervous. I was just preparing myself for a rescue mission when she broke the surface again. She held something out to me, treading water with her free arm.

I took the thing from her.

It was a nest.

Impossibly dry, impossibly beautiful. I put it in my lap. It was made of intricately woven twigs and pieces of cloth and hay and white feathers. My mother held the boat tightly and then lifted herself up and over the side.

"I made that," she said proudly.

"Mom—do you know what happened to Mary? Do

you know why she's turning into . . ."

It was hard to say it out loud: *a bird.*

My mother's face darkened. She shook her head.

"Is there any way to stop it?" I asked. "I sort of like her human."

"It's something she will have to learn how to control. Right now, she's not in control at all. Right now, we're lucky she doesn't just float away."

"But *why*?" I asked. "What could have happened to her?"

"I don't know," she said, her face darkening. "Something bad." She pulled the oar out of the ground and laid it across the boat. "You don't know who she was with that night?"

"We were together at the Fowl Fair," I said, thinking back. "And then she just kind of disappeared. Vira said—"

But I stopped, because I remembered what Vira had said that night, when I asked if she'd seen my sister: *I think she was talking to Peter earlier.* There wasn't anything unusual about that; Peter had a tendency of always being underfoot, especially when Mary was involved. But why hadn't I thought to ask him earlier, if he knew anything about where she had gone that night?

"What is it?" Mom asked.

"Maybe nothing," I said.

She began paddling toward the house. Harrison and Prue were waiting on the porch, watching us. Harrison helped Mom out of the boat. I stepped onto the porch;

Prue took my hand and touched the nest.

"Is that for the eggs?"

I nodded. "Will you take it to them?"

She took the nest from me and ran into the house.

"Excellent diving, Penelope," Harrison told my mother.

"Thank you, Harrison. And thank you for helping my daughter."

"Mom—can we borrow the rowboat?"

"Be my guest." She put her hands on either side of my head and kissed my forehead. "It comes from here," she said, and pointed to my belly. I felt a strange flutter where her fingers had touched but I had absolutely no idea what she was talking about. I smiled and nodded, which was always the safest response.

She swayed a little. Harrison reached a hand out and steadied her.

The effects of the magic she'd done. Strong magic; she was completely sapped.

"I'll just go lie down for a while," she said with a weak smile. She went into the house, and Harrison climbed into the boat.

"She found a nest in the water?" he asked.

"It's a long story."

"Magicky?"

"Very magicky."

We waited for Prue.

"All tucked in," she said when she finally came back.

"Do you guys want to go on a little trip?" I asked, gesturing toward the rowboat.

"Where to?" Harrison asked.

"Well, first, I want to make sure Vira's okay. Who knows how high the waters are down there. And after that . . . I think I need to go talk to Peter Elmhurst."

"I'm in," Prue said. She stepped gingerly into the boat. Harrison and I followed suit.

We started paddling for the town green.

The island was an unrecognizable, treacherous beast.

We passed a few people in boats (both actual boats and those of the makeshift variety: plastic storage containers, garbage cans, bathtubs, wooden wine barrels), but once they got close enough to see who we were (or who *I* was, more specifically) they paddled hurriedly in the other direction.

The entire first floor of the Montgomerys' building, including the Ice Cream Parlor facade, was underwater.

We steered the rowboat around to the back of the building, and I pulled myself onto the metal staircase. I promised Harrison and Prue I wouldn't take long, and then I knocked on Vira's front door.

She appeared a moment later, threw the door open, and squeezed me into a hug.

"I've been worried sick," she said. "It's getting bad out there."

"We found the eggs. And my sister is turning into a bird. We're going to talk to Peter. I think he might have been the last person to see her before whatever happened to her in the barn."

Vira took this news in stride.

She looked past me to where Prue and Harrison waited in the rowboat. "Is that your ride?" she asked.

"Yeah. It's a little slow, but it's all we have."

Vira put her hand over her eyes to shield them from the pouring water. She scanned the island, left to right, and then smiled.

"She's almost back. Just give me a second."

She went into the house and emerged a moment later in a bright-yellow raincoat covered in cheery cartoon ducks. She fit a matching hat on her head.

"Wow. I've never loved you this much," I said.

"And you're about to love me even more." She pointed over my shoulder. "Behold, our new ride."

I turned around to see Julia Montgomery pulling up to the second-floor railing of the building behind the wheel of a squat little red tugboat. Julia threw the lines to her daughter, and Vira tied the boat up. Julia stepped onto the landing.

"Georgina, it's so nice to see you," Julia said, and although her voice was a little strained, I thought she mostly meant it.

"Can we take the tug out? Errands," Vira said.

"Do I want to know what kind of errands?" Julia asked.

"We're going to clear my name," I offered. "And Mary's, while we're at it."

Julia considered for just a moment, and then she dropped the keys to the tugboat into Vira's waiting hands.

"Why does your mother own a tugboat?" I asked Vira as the four of us ditched the rowboat for our upgraded ride.

"Tugboats are really useful," Vira said, as if it were obvious, and then she pointed her chin at Prue and winked at me approximately eight hundred times.

"Okay, okay, you've made your point," I said.

She took her place as the captain of the tugboat, and it was like the universe shifted just a little bit back into place, as if to say, *Yes, of course this is where Elvira Montgomery belongs: behind the wheel of a tugboat wearing a matching raincoat and rainhat.*

Then she called, "I recommend life jackets! It's been a while since I've actually driven this thing," and that feeling shattered just a tiny bit. Harrison, Prue, and I dutifully slid into our bright-orange life vests (I helped Vira put hers on) and with a slightly worrying lurch, we were off.

We made our way to the Elmhursts' farm through water that was growing more and more unruly. The tugboat had been a lifesaver; there was no way we could have rowed ourselves through waves this high and choppy. Prue turned green and gripped the railing, keeping her head over the side of the boat, staring into the dark water like she might, at any given moment, hurl.

The rain had become a thing alive and dangerous, pouring down around us in buckets. It was impossible to see more than five or ten feet in front of the boat. Vira took it slow, and I stood at the bow with an actual lantern, feeling very 1800s-whale-hunting-expedition, yelling back to her if we came too close to buildings or trees sticking up out of the water. We found the Elmhursts' barn almost by accident, after weaving back and forth with no real idea of where we were.

The barn doors were open—the yellow police tape gone—and the water poured in and out of the entrance freely. Together with Harrison I guided the boat carefully through the doors. The lights were off—I wondered if the power outage had affected the whole island—but I held the lantern up and Harrison took his flashlight out again and pointed it around. The beam landed on Peter, sitting on the loft with his legs dangling over the side. The water was so high that the bottom of his sneakers skimmed the surface every time they kicked back and forth.

He had a strange expression on his face. I felt like I had stumbled upon him in a too-intimate moment.

Vira killed the engine of the tugboat.

Prue finally vomited.

Harrison rubbed her back.

The three of them presently occupied, I turned to Peter. "Hi," I said.

"Hey, Georgie," he replied.

"What are you doing in here?"

"I went for a little swim, but the water's too choppy now. I was waiting to see if it would go down."

"You went for a swim in your clothes?" I asked, because Peter was wearing jeans and a dark T-shirt and even a pair of sneakers, all sopping wet now.

"I figured—I was already soaked," he said lightly. "Why not?"

It actually made sense; what little time I'd spent in the storm since I'd changed my clothes had left me as dripping wet as Peter.

"And your parents? Are they okay? The water's getting high."

"They're fine," he replied, gesturing vaguely. "They found higher ground." Then he looked at me like he was seeing me for the first time. "What brings you over here, Georgie?"

"Peter, I wanted to ask you about the night of the Fowl Fair. Did you talk to my sister? Do you know where she went?"

"Has she said something?" he asked.

"Not really. She's . . . waiting out the storm," I said, because there was some edge to his voice, something that told me to choose my words carefully.

"I miss her," he admitted, and his face softened a little, and whatever strangeness I'd sensed in him just a moment ago vanished. He was Peter again. Peter the jack-of-all-trades. Peter the shy and quiet and in-love-with-my-sister boy.

"Do you know anything about that night?" I asked.

"Of course I do. But I love your sister, Georgina. I was trying to protect her."

"Protect her? From what?" My heart felt like someone held it in their hand, like someone was squeezing it tighter and tighter.

"Georgina," he said slowly. "Isn't it obvious?" He paused to rub at his eyes with wet hands. Then he looked at me again. "Mary killed Annabella."

And (oh timing, oh you silly, silly timing) the roof of the barn gave in under the weight of the rain.

Prue screamed as a piece of roofbeam, soggy and bloated with rain, came crashing down on the boat. The loft collapsed underneath Peter and he went plunging into the black water. I heard Vira shouting for a life preserver and before I could react, Harrison found one and threw it over the edge to Peter, who was struggling to stay afloat in water now riddled with debris. A massive piece of roof came plummeting down from the ceiling; I felt something crash into me, and the next thing I knew, Vira was on top of me, her face inches from mine.

"Did you just save my life?" I asked shakily.

"Thank me later," she said, scrambling to her feet and hoisting me up.

Peter was too far away to reach the life preserver; Harrison was struggling to pull it back into the boat so he could throw it farther. I grabbed the end of the rope and we pulled together, heaving as the boat pitched back and forth and sent us stumbling, more than once, to our knees.

Vira got behind the wheel again and the boat stuttered forward, dangerously close now to Peter, who flailed in the water and kept disappearing for longer and longer periods of time, getting weaker and weaker.

Harrison and I finally managed to haul the life preserver onto the boat, and he yelled back at Vira—"Hold her steady!"—before he grabbed it and dove headfirst into the water.

"Harrison!" Prue screamed from the back of the boat. She picked her way across bits of roof and beam that had landed on the boat, finally reaching me and half flinging herself over the railing. "Harrison!"

I grabbed on to the back of her lifejacket so she wouldn't pitch over the side, and we both searched the water for Harrison, who was paddling toward where Peter was struggling to stay afloat. When he reached him, Harrison slipped the life preserver over Peter's body and then used the rope to start pulling them back to the ship.

"In the stern!" Vira shouted over the rain. "There's a ladder in the stern!"

"Go around, Harrison!" Prue said, pointing frantically. She ran toward the back of the boat and made sure the ladder was extended. Harrison and Peter reached it after a moment and then they were on the deck, breathing heavily, Peter leaning over the side and retching water.

After a few more harrowing moments of navigating backward out of the barn, we were safe.

Well. *Safe* was relative.

I gave Peter a life jacket—he seemed shaken, but mostly unharmed—and Harrison found a compass in (of course) the pocket of his trench coat. We made our way slowly south, through squall-like winds and rain that came in sideways, soaking every part of my body, soaking even the *inside* of my body.

I wanted to grab Peter, shake him, ask him what he meant when he said that Mary killed Annabella, but I made myself take a deep breath and give him a minute to recover. Besides—my sister told me she hadn't done it. The Ouija board itself had said it was an *evil man*. I had to trust my sister.

But I couldn't deny, either, the newly formed smudge of doubt that had been born within me. A worm of evil that questioned my sister's story and her motives and her innocence. A worm that slithered its way through my body, slowly eating me from the inside out. That was what happened when you stopped trusting your sister, your twin: you were eaten alive in a gale, shivering and soaking and miserable.

And Mary had been acting so *weird*.

I had to get back to her.

Whatever she was doing in that tree, I had to make her tell me the truth.

And since it didn't seem likely that I'd be able to get to her *alone*, I'd take the compromise of me plus four others.

As it turned out, Prue wasn't quite done being sick.

She sat on the floor of the boat, her back pressed up against the aft side, her knees bent and a bucket between them. She was a pale green, the color of new grass. I left Harrison to navigate at the bow of the boat, and I went to sit next to her.

"I'm so sorry," I said.

"It's the back and forth," she said, illustrating with her hand. "It's the rocky-rocky. It's the—"

She paused to vomit.

When she was done, I helpfully tossed the contents overboard and handed the bucket back to her.

"Thanks," she said. She gripped it like a security blanket. "You must be really attracted to me right now."

"Surprisingly enough, I am."

"You don't believe him, do you?"

I paused just a moment too long, just a half a second, but it was enough time for Prue to see the worm inside me.

"The eggs," I whispered. "The feathers."

"Georgina, she's your *sister*," Prue said.

"But the whole island . . . Everybody's so sure . . ."

"Well, *I'm* not so sure. I'm not so sure at all," Prue

replied, and to punctuate this point, she vomited again.

The fierce loyalty of Prue made the worm shut up for a few seconds. I emptied the bucket again and then hugged her, kissing her wet hair and the side of her face.

"Georgina!" Vira called then, and I gave Prue back her bucket and joined the captain at her post. "Tree ho!" she said, and pointed. Then she turned back and saw how confused I looked. "It's like 'land ho,' but it's a tree. Tree ho. Get it? Because there's no more land; it's all water. Anyway, we're here."

My sister's tree. The water now reached halfway up its trunk; the tire swing was floating useless on the waves. Peter looked nervous; he stood up and did his best to pace with what limited deck space he had.

I climbed the tree again.

My sister was still a girl, sitting right where I'd left her. She was making a tiny nest in her lap with strips she'd torn from her dress and feathers she'd pulled from her hair and twigs she'd pilfered from the tree.

"Did you find them?" she asked.

The eggs.

"Yes, Mary."

"Are they safe?"

"They're safe. Mom made them a nest."

"Why did you bring him here?"

"Peter?"

"I told you I was hiding, and you brought him right to

me. I can't say I understand your approach," Mary said, and she sounded so much like herself that I wanted to cry.

But then I heard what she said, as if on a delay.

"Peter?" I asked. "You were hiding from *Peter*?"

"Why do you look like that?" She shook her head and laughed. "Wait—let me guess. Did he tell you I killed Annabella? That I used my magic powers to cut off his dick?" She rolled her eyes and in that moment I swear she grew taller. "I should have. I *wish* I had dick-chopping magic powers."

"Mary?"

She shrank again.

She closed her eyes, squeezed her eyelids together.

When she opened them again, I saw real fear there.

"Why did you bring him here?" she whispered.

And on the bough of this tree, in the middle of a gale, with my sister so small and fragile in front of me, I could suddenly see—with such sharp clarity it made me squint—how dense I'd been.

My sister hadn't killed Annabella.

Of course my sister hadn't killed Annabella.

But I knew who did.

Evil man.

"What did he do to you?" I asked.

But I already knew.

And I was already climbing back down the tree.

And I was already back on the boat.

And I was already throwing myself at Peter, who looked suddenly terrified, caught, *guilty.*

I felt Harrison grab my arm and pull me back.

"Georgina?" he said. "What's going on?"

I stopped fighting.

The four of us—Prue, Harrison, Vira, me—were at the bow of the boat.

Peter backed up and up until he was at the very back.

Harrison let go of my arm.

"Tell me what you did to my sister," I whispered.

And the minute the words left my mouth—

The minute they touched the air—

The rain stopped.

BIRTHDAY

Everything suddenly felt very, very clear.

"Tell me what you did to my sister," I repeated, and Peter put his hands up in front of him like I was threatening to shoot.

"What did she tell you?" Prue asked, moving to my side, slipping her hand in mine. "What did he do?"

"He has to say it. I want to hear him say it."

Peter looked terrified.

I remembered Peter as a child, playing tag with Mary and me in the backyard of the inn. I remembered Peter red-faced and mumbling at the beginning of the season, asking me if Mary had gotten the letter he'd written to her, the sharp flicker of anger on his face that he'd quickly gotten under control. I remembered Peter stacking wood for countless summer fires in the backyard of the inn. There was no appropriate place in my mind for the version of

Peter that was currently forming there.

Above us, a bolt of lightning streaked across the sky. Prue jumped and let go of my hand.

"Tell me, Peter," I said.

"You better talk, asshole," Vira chimed in. "It's four against one."

"I have no idea what you're talking about," Peter said. "Look, we went to the barn after the Fowl Fair. We fell asleep. When I woke up—she was standing over the bird, okay? She killed the bird; I saw her throw it against the beam. I'm the innocent one here. You should be interrogating *her*."

I took one tiny step toward Peter.

Above us, a low rumble of thunder.

"I don't believe you," I said.

"I'm telling you the truth," Peter insisted. "And there's more. I saw her *fly*. Everything they say about your family is true, and I'm going to tell everyone. Who do you think they'll believe? Me? Or a *Fernweh*."

He said the word like it was a swear, like something dark and twisted. He said the word like it was a stone that fell out of his mouth and shattered into bloodred crystals on the floor. He said the word exactly like he was saying another word entirely. He said the word like he was actually saying the word—

Slut.

All of the pieces of that night were shifting and clicking

into place inside my brain. My sister's torn shirt. The bruise in the bathtub. My sister's broken necklace. My sister's nightmares. My sister's terror.

Peter saw it.

Peter saw everything that I knew about him, and he was suddenly scared of it.

Good.

Let him be scared.

"Georgina," he whispered. "You *know* me."

"I know my sister," I countered.

"I would never do anything to . . ."

But the lie was too big for him to even say.

Because he *had* hurt my sister.

I took another step toward him.

He held his hands up in front of him. Like he could stop me.

His face changed.

A shadow passed over his features, and I saw him how my sister must have seen him that night in the barn, that night when she said *no* and he said *yes*.

"Do you have any idea," he began, his words dipped in acid, "what it's felt like, all these years, watching your sister go out and . . ."

He put his hands over his face. His shoulders bounced in some silent, hate-filled laugh.

"I *loved* her," he said. "I wrote her letters and brought her presents and walked her home in the dark and made her tea and left flowers on her bed. I did *everything* for her, and do you know how it's felt to watch her pick every single guy on this island except *me*?"

His eyes were flashing now.

The sky had turned a deep, dark purple. The lightning split the clouds in half and set the whole world on fire. Someone put a hand on my arm, and when I tried to brush it off, whoever it was just held on tighter.

I turned around.

Mary.

Out of the tree and (thank God, thank God, thank God) still a girl.

"Let's just go home," she said. "It isn't worth it."

"Go *home*?"

"He's right, Georgina. This is why I didn't tell you. Nobody's going to believe me. Everybody knows I'm a . . ."

Fernweh.

Bitch.

Slut.

"That's bullshit," I spat. Another crack of lightning, a flash so bright we all paused and looked upward.

When I looked back at Mary, her mouth was open just a little. She was staring at me.

"Oh my God," she said.

"What?"

"This whole time," she said.

"Mary, *what*?"

She grabbed my hand. She pointed up at the sky.

It had started to rain again. Tiny drops of ice-cold water.

Mary stopped pointing at the sky and pointed, instead, at my face.

"Georgina, you're crying," she said.

It felt like time was moving only for my sister and me. Everyone else on the boat stood silent and still, frozen, suspended.

"So?" I said, and wiped at my cheeks. "What's your point? I always cry when it rains; you always say that."

Mary smiled. "It's the other way around," she said. "It always rains when you cry."

"That's the same thing."

"It's not the same thing at all. Don't you see?" she said. "It's your *thing*, Georgina. This is your thing. It's *always* been your thing; it was just too big for any of us to see!"

Mary had both my hands in both her hands, and she was smiling for the first time in days, in weeks, in who could tell how long in this timeless, broken summer. I looked down at the floor; her feet were hovering an inch or two above the wooden planks of the tugboat. "Happy birthday," she said.

And then Prue screamed.

And the world around Mary and me came unpaused and leapt into motion.

I turned around.

And Peter had a gun, an old and tarnished pistol that he

held like a thing he did not know how to hold, gripped in two hands so tightly that his arms shook with the effort, the almost-imperceptible quivers that radiated up to his elbows, his shoulders, his chest. His lips had turned white. He looked almost as scared of the gun as we were.

"Peter, what are you doing?" I asked.

He tightened his grip. I imagined Peter sneaking into his parents' room, taking this gun from his father's nightstand, trying to figure out if it was loaded.

I wondered why Peter thought he might need a gun.

I wondered if he guessed I would find out eventually.

Behind me I heard Vira whisper, "Evil man."

"Just put it down, Peter. Don't be like this," I said.

"No way. I don't know what you two are capable of," he said, almost frantically, gesturing between Mary and me like we were bombs instead of girls.

"Surely no more than what *you* were capable of," I said.

"If you just let me go, if you just . . . I'll go home, and I won't even tell anyone what she did. I won't even tell anybody," Peter said.

"What *I* did?" Mary repeated. "I didn't do anything, Peter. All I did was say *no*."

"You make yourself sound so innocent," he snapped. "Did you tell them how *you* were the one who wanted to go to the barn in the first place? How *you* were the one to start it all?"

"And how you threw Annabella against the beam when

I wouldn't go further? And about how I started screaming, and how you put your hands over my mouth so I'd shut up, and about how you climbed on top of me? How you told me what you would do to me if I told anyone . . ."

Mary covered her face with her hands.

I imagined my sister, broken and violated, slipping Annabella's eggs into her pocket so Peter wouldn't hurt them. I imagined my sister saying the word *no*. I imagined my sister shrinking, shrinking . . .

Peter held the gun in his sweating, shaking hands.

Could guns fire after they'd been soaked in floodwater?

"Peter, just put the gun down," I said.

"No. No way," Peter said, and he tightened his grip.

For the first time in my life I felt the power of the Fernweh women, ready and waiting at my fingertips.

Exactly like my mother had said: a burning, tight feeling in my gut.

Next to me, my sister shrank. And shrank.

Prue and Vira and Harrison were completely silent and motionless behind me.

I had never really given much thought about what my eighteenth birthday might look like. There'd be cake, sure. There'd be a colorful banner strung across the dining room: *Happy Birthday!* There'd be Mary and my mother and a quiet dinner. A bonfire in the backyard maybe, a small pile of presents wrapped in brown paper and twine.

I'd never considered the possibility of that summer

leading me here: standing on a boat, a gun aimed at my chest and my sister sprouting feathers next to me, long shiny feathers that erupted out of her skin at an alarming rate.

I made myself not look at her.

It seemed private, somehow, this moment of transformation. It seemed like my sister's business.

I focused my attention on Peter.

I knew that he would use that gun, because that is what small, scared men did: they used things more powerful than themselves to make up the difference. They hid behind weapons of mass destruction: big guns and bigger bombs.

They were small, small, small—

Peter was small, but I could see him becoming bigger in his own mind as his finger inched toward the trigger.

"I'm giving you one last chance," I said.

He laughed. "*You're* giving *me* a last chance? I'm the one with the gun!"

And I watched as his finger wrapped around the trigger.

And I lifted my hand into the sky.

And I didn't know quite how I did it, only that the tightness in my belly was moving upward. A tightness that demanded to be released.

And I raised my hand higher—

And the skies opened up—

And the skies poured down—

And I heard a loud *crack*—the loudest of cracks—the
crack of an old evil gun held by a young evil man—
    And the flash lit up the entire world—
    And everything went white.

AFTER

I woke up in my bed.

The world was dark.

There was a bandage wrapped around my head, covering my eyes.

I started to unwind it, but I felt my mother lay her hand on my wrist.

Call it a Fernweh thing or a daughter thing; I knew my mother's hand even with bandages wrapped so thickly around my eyes that the light couldn't even peek around the edges.

"Easy," she said. "Close your eyes."

I closed my eyes underneath the bandage. My mother's hands started to unravel it for me. My mother's hands were steady, cool things, and I could feel them trembling through the thin fabric.

When she slipped the bandage off, she put one palm over my eyes.

"Give it time," she said.

Without the bandage, even with my eyes closed and my mother's fingers blocking the sun, the world seemed so, so bright. My eyes ached with it.

"What happened?" I asked.

"Don't you remember?"

"Is Mary okay?"

"Are *you* okay?"

"Are you going to answer every question with a question?" I said, and gently pulled her hand away.

The insides of my eyelids were a bright, painful red.

"Has the sun exploded?" I asked.

"I imagine if the sun had exploded, we wouldn't be around to comment on it."

"There was a bright flash."

"Yes . . . ," my mother answered, prodding for more.

"I thought that might have been what it was. The sun exploding."

"Not quite."

I still had my eyes squeezed shut. I tried opening them the tiniest crack. My bedroom was a blurry, bright mess through the crosshatched black lines of my eyelashes. I shut them again. My head throbbed.

"I don't feel so great."

"You've exerted a fair amount of energy. On your very first try. You've been asleep for a long time. It doesn't surprise me that you don't feel well."

"I remember . . ."

"Yes?"

"He had a gun," I said. Suddenly that was the only thing I could see: Peter holding a gun. What was Peter doing with a gun?

Peter saying the word *Fernweh*.

Peter meaning the word *slut*.

Prue screaming.

Vira, the captain of a tugboat.

Harrison pulling flashlight after flashlight from a trench coat with impossibly deep pockets.

It came back to me in fits and starts, flashes and snapshots.

I opened my eyes again. Slowly. The light felt like an invasive, heavy thing. My mother was blurry.

I had raised my hand up toward the sky and called a bolt of lightning down from the heavens.

"Just like fucking Zeus," I whispered.

"Ah, so you're remembering," Mom said.

"Holy shit. Did I kill him?"

Peter had forced himself on my sister in a gross, dusty barn, and Peter had thrown a three-hundred-year-old bird against a wooden beam and snapped her wings and neck, and Peter had aimed a gun at my face, but—despite all that—I didn't think I was prepared to add *murderer* to the list of attributes I used to describe myself.

"Not quite," my mother said. Her face came slowly into focus, and I saw how sad she looked, how tired.

"I think I was trying to."

"Oh, you were certainly trying to. But luckily you have three very eager witnesses who've all given testimony in your favor. Plus, the gun was found. Albeit a little worn for the wear."

"Worn for the wear?"

"Your aim was very precise. Your . . . how did you put it? Your Zeus bolt hit the gun."

"So he's alive."

"I said *a little* worn for the wear; I think I should amend that to *a lot* worn for the wear," my mother said thoughtfully. "He was blown into next Tuesday. Really. I had to go and drag him back to the present. He smokes when he opens his mouth and he's covered in burns, but he'll live."

"He fired the gun," I said.

"Yes."

"He tried to kill me."

"You were very lucky."

"You knew," I said. "You must have. You knew I was making it rain."

"I had a feeling it was you, yes."

"When did you figure it out? Have you known all along?"

The storm when I was born. The snow in summer. The blazing heat in the dead of winter. The weather of By-the-Sea had always been laughably temperamental.

But no—not always.

Just for the last eighteen years. Because of me.

"Not all along," my mother admitted. "Not for a while. No Fernweh woman has ever had this particular gift before. I didn't know what to look for."

"And then? When you realized it? How come you didn't tell me?"

But I already knew what she was going to say.

I had to come to it when I was ready.

As if she could read my mind (and who knows, stranger things had happened), she kissed me on the forehead and said, "Exactly."

"What will happen to Peter?"

"You don't have to worry about Peter. He'll be going to jail for a long time."

"There will be a trial?"

"Of course."

"But who's going to believe him over us? Who's going to believe him over Mary?"

"Like I said, Georgina, you have witnesses. And that young Harrison Lowry has proved to be quite the advocate on your and Mary's behalf. We'll make sure Peter's punishment matches his crimes."

My mother's eyes darkened.

We hadn't said the word yet.
Words had power.
Just like the words—
Slut.
Magic.
Fernweh.
They had power.
So did the word—
Rape.

BIRD

In the bright flash of a bolt of lightning called down from the sky by magic I never knew I possessed—

My sister had disappeared.

I remembered now.

The smell of burning flesh.

The light so bright it had washed the entire world away.

The tiny flutter on my shoulder.

Like the smallest, most delicate little body had landed there for just a moment—

Before flying away.

As if to say—

Thank you.

LEAVING

The island drained of water as I lay recovering in my bed.
 It ran off over the cliffs in dramatic waterfalls.
It drained into the sea.
The ground was soggy underfoot.
But we knew it would dry eventually.
Peter enjoyed a swift trial with a jury of his peers, who convicted his raping, bird-murdering, illegal-possession-of-a-firearm, attempted-murdering-of-a-human ass to fourteen years in prison. He also had to register as a sex offender. He was shipped to the mainland on the next ferry out.
His defense—*she deserved it because she had already had sex with so many people*—made the judge, the Honorable Eleanora Avery, laugh the fuck out loud.
As if out of a fairy tale, nobody asked:
What was my sister wearing the night she was raped?

How much had my sister had to drink the night she was raped?

How many guys had my sister previously had sex with?

Because—again, out of a fairy tale—they realized that none of those things mattered.

Because there was nothing in a girl's history that might negate her right to choose what happens to her body.

The last days of summer settled into a quiet rhythm.

The island was hot and humid and somber.

I spent the days washing the sheets and pillowcases and towels of the inn, preparing for the end of the season, getting ready for fall. I spent my evenings with Prue— pushing ourselves out into nothingness on a tire swing or running full speed into the ocean or lying on the cool grass of dusk, flicking mosquitoes from our skin and letting our hair tangle up together.

I woke up every morning and went into the kitchen and poured myself a cup of coffee.

Aggie laughed again. The inn became a place I recognized.

I let the birdheads apologize, one by one, a steady stream of humiliated people I had known my entire life.

I forgave everyone who asked me to.

I said to good-bye to them, one by one, these people who had dedicated their lives to a thing that had been so violently taken from them.

I watched them lay their hands on the top of Annabella's grave.

I watched them pull the grave marker out of the

earth—the one Peter had made—and fling it into the sea.

The rule of the cliffs did not apply to grave markers carved by rapists.

Our good-byes were short and perfunctory (Hep Shackman) or long and drawn out (Lucille Arden) depending on who was leaving.

Liesel Channing gave me a sweater she had knit out of truly hideous purple yarn. On the front was a rather sloppily rendered crest of the university I was slated to attend so soon that it took my breath away when I thought too much about it. She hugged me for a very long time and whispered in my ear, "I'll be back next year. Annabella or no Annabella, this is my home too."

Every morning I went into my sister's empty, quiet room and checked on the eggs.

The nest, magically rendered and pulled from the flooded ground under a full moon, kept them warm and safe under the floorboards.

We took turns watching over them: Harrison, Prue, Vira, me. We stacked books and magazines on Mary's bed and read stories and watched Annabella's babies.

I thought it was too late for them.

Vira told me that they had a magic nest to help them along, and I should have a little hope.

When I missed my sister, I held her necklace in the palm of my hand. The broken clasp told an entirely different story now.

I wondered if I should have seen it earlier.

I listed all the reasons a girl might have to keep something like that a secret, even from her own sister.

I went through the motions of leaving.

I packed my things into three steamer trunks.

I got a letter in the mail with my future roommate's name and address.

Hattie M. Hipperson.

I sent her a letter.

Excited to meet you.
Excited for school.
Excited.

(The word *excited* falls flatter and flatter the more times you write it.)

And then—through some trick of time, a slow bleeding of hours—it was the day before I was supposed to leave.

I woke up and poured myself a cup of coffee and brought it up to Mary's room.

Vira was already there.

Vira, too, was getting ready to leave By-the-Sea for her own rumspringa. She was going to a big city on the opposite coast, the western coast, a city full of sun and palm trees and surfer boys and long-haired girls she could care two shits about. When I pictured Vira in a midnight-black bikini standing with her feet in sand almost too hot to bear, I wanted to cry tears of absolute joy. Like Vira in a candy-striped apron scooping ice cream the color of rusted nails, like Vira at the wheel of a tugboat in a yellow raincoat, like Vira, my best friend, whose house was covered in roadkill taxidermy—it just made so much sense.

I suspected that Vira, of the vampire name and the no-fucks-given attitude, had it all figured out in a way I could only one day hope to.

I sat on my sister's bed and threw my arms around Vira's shoulders. She put her hands on my forearms and said, "I'm going to miss you so much. But you can be from my school to your school in five hours. Flying through the air! What will they think of next?"

We stayed like that for a while, me hugging her, her patting my arms, the eggs out of their cubby hole, resting on the floor of Mary's closet.

After a few minutes I realized that Vira was humming. And then her humming turned into words: a familiar eerie tune that filled the room with its simple, somber melody.

On By-the-Sea, you and me will go sailing by
On waves of green, softly singing too.
On By-the-Sea, you and me will be forever young
And live together on waves of blue.

I thought I saw the eggs twitch, but when I looked closer, they were still.

"We're leaving tomorrow too," Prue told me that evening.

There was one ferry off the island per day (ever since it had miraculously recovered from its mysterious ailment) and the very idea of getting onto it with Prue by my side made things seem suddenly a million times more bearable.

But still.

When I tried to actually picture myself leaving By-the-Sea, I couldn't.

All the signs pointed to me leaving.

The packed steamer trunks.

The envelope of money my mother had tucked into my hands that morning, for me to open my very own bank account once I reached the mainland. (*The By-the-Sea Bank doesn't count for much off these shores,* she'd said.)

The week's worth of food Aggie had packed carefully into a wicker picnic basket. (*For the journey,* she'd said, although there was more than enough food for one ferry ride and one train ride.)

My ferry ticket.

My train ticket.

The response from my roommate, Hattie M. Hipperson, who somehow managed to seem much more sincere every time she wrote the word *excited* in her letter back to me. (Which was seventeen times in four neatly printed pages.)

The thick black knitted hat Julia Montgomery had made for me and delivered that afternoon, with matching gloves and scarf for good measure. (*"The winters get so cold in that city, Georgina,"* she'd said, and hugged me for so long that it began to feel less like a hug and more like an extended apology.)

The feather I found on my pillow that night, the beautiful pale-brown feather placed perfectly where I would later lay my head.

The magical nest in my sister's room that somehow, between watches of its diligent guardians, had gone empty. Not a piece of egg nor fluff of feather left to be found.

I put the nest in Mary's nightstand drawer.

I didn't worry about the eggs; I knew they were in good hands.

I woke up that night to my sister hovering over me.

She clamped her hand down over my mouth before I could scream and then she fell, laughing, to the bed.

"You should have seen your face," she squealed.

"Am I dreaming?"

"Don't be a doofus. Did you really think I turned into a *bird*?"

"Sort of, yeah," I admitted.

"Well, yeah, I sort of did," she admitted back.

"You took the eggs?"

"Yeah. Don't worry. They're safe." She snuggled under

the blankets with me. "I heard about Peter."

"He got what he deserved."

"You should have killed him," she said. Then, worried she'd hurt my feelings, she added, "Just kidding, of course. He wouldn't have been worth the extra energy."

"Mary, why didn't you tell me?" I asked.

Her face darkened, and she wiggled herself deeper under the blankets, pulling them over our heads so we were totally covered.

"I was afraid nobody would believe me," she whispered, her voice soft and muffled by wool.

"*I* would have believed you. I will always believe you."

"This island, Georgie . . . ," she began. "This island is so small. People talk. I hear what they say about me. The whispers. I've heard them call me things. They would have said I was asking for it."

In the darkness, I reached out for her and put my index finger on the tip of her nose.

"I'm sorry this happened to you. And I'm sorry I didn't figure it out before," I said.

"You don't have to be sorry for anything. You saved my life, remember? You pulled a lightning bolt down from the sky like fucking *Zeus*."

"I think that was mostly an accident."

"You blew Peter to kingdom come! Honestly, who cares if it was an accident or not."

"I should have known. Mary, I'm so sorry I didn't know."

"I thought about telling you," she said, her voice a whisper again. "Maybe I should have. I just felt so lost, so confused. I felt like I didn't know which way was up anymore, which way was *right*. Whether I *had* done something. To deserve it."

"I love you. I'm sorry. I hope you know now that you didn't do anything."

"I know," she said quickly. "You have to stop apologizing to me; it's not your fault. And you need to snap out of this mood, because the island's been gray as shit the past couple of days, and I know it's because you've been moping around."

"I'm leaving tomorrow."

"I know that too. I know everything. I can fit into really small places now. I can just listen."

"So you *are* a bird?"

"Details are unimportant." She paused, lifted the blankets a little so we could breathe, so a sliver of light found its way into the bed. She looked sad and small with the covers pulled up over her head and our faces inches apart. Her breath smelled like tea and rain. "I heard something," she said. "A secret."

"What kind of secret?"

"Did you know," she said, fiddling with the collar of

my pajama shirt, "that no Fernweh woman has ever left the island before?"

"What? Where did you hear that?"

"I was hiding in the eaves. I was *literally* eavesdropping."

"And?"

"It's true. Mom and Aggie were talking. I knew Mom had never left the island, and Grandma, but I didn't realize *none* of us . . ."

"Well, I guess that's going to change. Because I'm leaving the island tomorrow. And you."

Again, in the darkness, Mary was quiet.

"Poor Mildred Miller," she whispered. "Robbed of the distinct pleasure of sharing a very small cinder block dorm room with me."

"You're not going? Because of what Mom and Aggie said?"

"It feels like I was never going," Mary whispered. "And it doesn't have anything to do with . . . Peter or what happened or . . . There are just some things I need to do now. Here."

"Like what?"

"Like, I dunno. Could you actually picture me at college? Could you picture me away from this weird little island? Plus, it looks like I'm going to have to raise some babies."

"You aren't talking about the eggs, are you?"

"Of course I am. Although if those little fuckers think

I'm going to chew worms and then vomit them back up, they're sadly misinformed about how far I'll take my maternal hen duties."

"Disgusting."

"Yeah, well. Somebody's gotta do it."

She stretched herself out on the bed, taking up all the room. I kissed the side of her face, and she pretended to barf.

"I'm going to miss you so much," I said.

"Don't worry. I can *fly*. I'll come and visit."

Mary was gone in the morning.

I thought I might actually scream if I found one more feather in my bed, but . . .

Nothing.

I got dressed and left the house early. The ferry left at noon, but I had one little thing left to do.

The island was quiet and warm in the soft morning light. I filled a thermos with coffee and set out down Bottle Hill wearing my rainboots, even though the ground was dry and hard by now. The island was back to its usual self, heavy with the thick heat of another summer's end, a mugginess that could be picked up in your palms and saved for a later day. I filled my pockets with it and kept walking.

Oh, By-the-Sea—how the place you grew up could feel at once so safe and so much like a trap. I had never wanted to leave it, but here I was, my bags packed and my good-byes all ready and waiting in the back of my throat.

"I'm not abandoning you," I whispered to the island, my island, but of course it didn't respond. Islands were like that. Always listening. Never replying.

The graveyard was orange and crisp and autumn as usual. I slipped a fleece button-down on and wandered through the graves. It was the place I'd miss most, I knew. The always-autumn graveyard.

And although I knew now that I must have been the one controlling the weather, I had no idea how I might reverse the effects.

Not that I wanted to.

It had always been perfect, this graveyard. It had always been empty and autumn and mine.

And now I was leaving it.

Who knew how long this rumspringa might last? I guess that was the point, sort of. A jump into the unknown with your hands pressed over your eyes.

I settled myself down in between the graves, crossing my legs and cupping my hands around the thermos to warm them. I thought of rain, of wind, of sunshine, of rainbows. All these things that suddenly felt like they might actually be a part of me in a way that felt huge, unfathomable.

I had brought a flood to By-the-Sea—

But had it been the first time?

The Fernweh mausoleum was the largest in the grave-yard. The outside was carved in Annabellas, a tribute to Annabella Fernweh and her sister, Georgina, my great-great-great-great-whatever-grandmother who had been among the first people to inhabit By-the-Sea. I bent down and found the loose stone near the door and removed the little key we kept hidden there.

When Mary and I were younger, we'd play in here. A morbid setting for our dolls to have teatime, but we had liked the stone floors and the way the light turned into rainbows from the stained-glass windows.

I found my father's empty tomb. There was nothing inside this stone container, no earthly remains of Locke Caravelle. His name wasn't even etched into the door. My mother wouldn't allow it. But this is where my father would go, should anyone ever find his body. This is where all the Fernweh women and the men who loved them were buried.

I put my palm against the cool stone.

I had heard the story a hundred times. The story of our birth. Of the final push that delivered me into the world, the push that coincided with the skies opening up. An island flooding around my mother and me as we waited for my sister to show up.

The great storm of our births—the one that had sunk my father's ship.

It had started the moment I was born.

And now I knew that my father's ship had gone down because of me.

My father's tomb was empty because of me.

I would never know my father because I was born with a power I didn't even want, one I didn't even know about for eighteen years.

And now I had it, and there was no sending it back. There was only going forward, and living with the knowledge that the newborn tears of baby Georgina had done so much more damage than anyone had realized at the time.

I wouldn't forget that. This power had blood on its hands.

"I'm so sorry," I whispered to his empty tomb.

"I'm so sorry," I whispered to all the women who had come before me.

And then I left them alone and promised I'd return one day.

The dead loved promises; the living loved promising.

I returned home and stood in my bedroom and turned in a slow circle, looking.

The day had turned bright and sunny.

I guess that meant I was in a good mood.

I had almost no clue how my powers worked. That

little knot of warmth in my gut—when I'd Zeused-out on Peter—that was gone.

If I stood at my window—

And looked up at the sky—

And concentrated very, very hard . . .

I could almost make a cloud appear.

"You'll figure it out," my mom said at the door to my bedroom. She was dressed less conspicuously now that all the birdheads were gone. Jeans and sneakers, a Smashing Pumpkins T-shirt. Her hair was in a long, straight ponytail and she held a cup of coffee, which she offered to me.

"Just coffee?" I asked, taking it.

"You're leaving me for nine months. You think I'm not going to make you a little protection spell?" she responded. We sat on my bed, facing each other.

"Mary came to see me last night."

"Me too," she said.

"She was a human."

My mom nodded. "She's not leaving."

"She told me."

"But I'm glad you are," Mom continued. "If it was going to be anyone . . ."

"Am I really the first? Out of all the Fernweh women?"

Mom nodded again.

Then: "You'll be great, Georgina. You've always been great. Since the minute you were born, sending floods after your enemies." She stared off into space, as if savoring the memory: her and Aggie and my sister and me in a wooden rowboat, making our way safely home.

Without my dad.

I couldn't imagine leaving her.

I couldn't imagine leaving this place.

And yet.

I went to say good-bye to Annabella.

My mother had made her a new grave marker. A flat little rock worn smooth from the ocean. Magically engraved words read: *We loved with a love that was more than love.*

And I thought—

In a million years, if some archaeologists unearthed the remains of By-the-Sea from the bottom of the seafloor (an Atlantis for a distant generation!), and found this rock with these words guarding these tiny, fragile bird bones, they would have no fucking idea what to make of us.

And that was fine with me.

With Aggie and Harrison's help, I loaded my three steamer trunks and one picnic basket into the bed of my mother's pickup. Harrison and Prue added their luggage, and I remembered, so vividly, the moment they'd gotten out of Seymore Stanners's taxi in the driveway of the inn, two months and an entire lifetime ago.

There's one for both of us, my sister had said.

But I'd promised myself I wouldn't cry (mostly because I really didn't want it to rain on all my stuff), and so I pushed that memory down somewhere to save until later.

"Are you okay?" Prue asked me.

"I'm okay," I said, and kissed her.

We lay down in the truck's bed as my mother drove us to the docks, watching the whitest, puffiest clouds crash against each other in the sky over what had been my entire world, what *would* be my entire world, at least for the next thirty minutes.

I closed my eyes and let the roar of the wind rush over me, drowning out as much as I could.

Everything would be okay.

The birdheads would come back.

The inn would stay open.

My sister was alive, and Peter was in jail.

The sun was shining.

And Prue was holding my hand.

You couldn't ask for much more than that.

I'd seen the ferry before, of course, many times, but somehow, today, it looked smaller.

"Are you sure this thing is seaworthy?" I whispered to my mother.

"I vomited twenty-seven times on the way over," Prue

said, overhearing me, dragging her suitcase out of the back of the truck. "But I survived."

"You're going on a great adventure," my mother said.

"Oh no. Are you going to cry?"

"Fernwehs don't cry," she said quickly, wiping at her cheeks.

Without warning, she threw her arms around me and hugged me so tightly I couldn't breathe.

When she let go, she was not crying, but her eyes were wet and red.

"I'll write to you every day," she said. "I'll even use a telephone. You know how much I hate the phone."

"And email?"

"And smoke signals, and carrier pigeons," she added. She kissed the tips of her fingers and then pressed them against my cheek.

"I love you."

"I love you too."

She got back in the truck but didn't drive away. I saw her shoulders shaking, her hands covering her face.

"Georgina? Are you ready?" Harrison asked.

I hadn't thanked him for everything he'd done, for showing up at Peter's trial and speaking out for my sister and for believing me without so much as a moment's hesitation.

"Harrison," I began.

He held his hand up. "It doesn't need to be said."

"But you did so much."

"Not any more than any decent birdhead should have done."

"Then I guess you're the only decent birdhead."

"Nah, cut 'em some slack. They're old. And mass hysteria is a dangerous drug. Let's not forget Salem." Then, darkening, "That probably wasn't the best parallel I could have made."

"An apt one, though. A literal you-know-what hunt."

"I'll never let them burn you at the stake," he said, and bowed to me, and I added *person who bows to other people* to my growing list of things I knew about Harrison Lowry.

Harrison and Prue started up the gangway from the dock to the boat. I followed afterward, but only made it halfway up before I heard my name being shrieked at a deafening pitch from behind me.

I turned.

Vira, of course, leaping off a bright-yellow bicycle and running toward me with her arms out and wide. She flung herself into me so hard we fell backward on the gangway.

"Did you think I wouldn't come and see you off, you *ass*?" she shrieked, hugging me tighter and tighter. "I'm going to miss you so much. You're like my favorite person in the entire world. Okay? Okay, Georgina?"

"Okay, okay! I love you too, Vira."

Vira climbed backward off me and kneeled there, her eyes so wide and her face so beautiful that I wanted to put her on pause, pull out a canvas and easel, and paint her picture right there in bright and beautiful oil paint, the last memory I'd have of her on By-the-Sea for who knew how long.

"You *can't* love Hattie M. Hipperson more than me," she whispered.

"Elvira, don't be ridiculous," I said.

"Call me as soon as you get there."

"Of course I will."

"I'll be sitting by the phone."

"Even before my mother."

"Okay," she said, breathing deep, trying not to cry. "Don't shoot anybody else with lightning bolts unless they *really* deserve it."

"I promise."

"Oh! I brought this for you," she said. She fished around in the folds of her coat and withdrew a small black journal, pressing it into my hands urgently. "Don't forget me. Don't forget anything. Write it all down."

"Do you really think I'm going to forget you, Vira?"

She didn't answer, but she squeezed my hands so hard they turned white. And then she kissed my cheek and helped me up and she ran down the gangway and I knew she wouldn't look back, I knew she'd jump on her bike and peddle away as fast as she could.

And she did.

Prue was waiting for me at the top of the gangway. She

was smiling so wide and—honestly, was *everybody* on the verge of tears?

"I wish I had a friend like that," she said.

"You have me."

"You're lucky, Georgina. This whole world is yours." And she pointed out across the island just as the gangway was lowered back onto the pier and the boat sounded two enormous horns and we pulled away from the dock.

My mother waved violently from the window of the pickup.

I waved back—

Until I couldn't see her anymore.

And then I saw them.

Three little birds, flying recklessly over the strong ocean wind, flying right toward the boat.

Three Annabellas.

One a little bigger.

Two little babies, just testing out their wings.

Learning how to fly.

And I waved to my sister too—

Until I couldn't see her either.

And then I sat down at a table inside the ferry's open cabin. And while Prue and Harrison ordered lunch from a little old lady who worked the concession stand, I opened the journal Vira had given me.

I found a pen in my bag.

And before I could forget—because it was even now

fading from my senses, it was even now too far away to properly identify—I wrote:

> On the island of By-the-Sea
> you could always smell
> two things:
> salt and magic.

ACKNOWLEDGMENTS

Every ninety-eight seconds, an American is sexually assaulted.

One in six women has been the victim of a rape or an attempted rape.

One in thirty-three men has been the victim of a rape or an attempted rape.

Transgender, genderqueer, and nonconforming individuals are at a much greater risk of sexual assault.*

---

*Statistics were provided by www.rainn.org. To reach the free, confidential, and 24-7 National Sexual Assault Hotline, call 1-800-656-HOPE.

This book is first and foremost for every single person who has been the victim of sexual violence.

To the people who had a direct hand in the making and shaping of this book, I could not possibly thank you enough, not even if I were to buy you a pint of every flavor of ice cream offered in Skull & Cone.

For sound advice, solid wisdom, and a great partnership that gives me confidence every single day, thank you to my agent, Wendy Schmalz.

To my family for their persistent support of everything I do and for having faith in me even when I fail to find that same faith in myself. And especially to Elliot, Alma, and Harper, who continue to be just the best-ever spots of light in my life.

To the real-life Georgina and the real-life Mary, thank you for lending your names to this book, but more importantly, thank you for always being two of the first readers of anything I write, and for always being honest and forthcoming in your feedback. And thanks for being two of the dearest friends I have—I am lucky to know you.

For the brilliant lending of many puns for this book (Skull & Cone, Fowl Fair, some others that got cut from the book but not from my heart) and for willing to stress text with me whenever I feel certain I'm going to abandon writing and become a long-distance trucker, I owe heaps of debt to Aaron Karo.

To my team at HarperTeen for standing behind me for

FOUR books (!!), and especially to my editor, Jocelyn Davies, for fielding all my questions and ideas and comments and concerns with only grace and care.

To the readers who have been with me since the very first book and put endless energy into promoting, sharing, blogging, tweeting, photographing, Instagramming, smoke signaling, yodeling, etc., etc. just to get the word out about my writing. Especially to Molly, Crini, Sana, Catherine, and Alice, who have been among the loudest and loveliest.

To Sandra Bullock's and Nicole Kidman's hair in *Practical Magic*. This book would frankly not have been written without it.

And to Shane, for everything and for always.